Forget your troubles,
Let go your woe.
Live for today 'cause
you might be dead come tomorrow!

ANNA
AND THE
APOCALYPSE

KATHARINE TURNER
WITH BARRY WALDO

Based on the
Screenplay by
ALAN McDONALD
AND RYAN McHENRY

[Imprint]
MAKE YOUR MARK

NEW YORK

[Imprint]
MAKE YOUR MARK

A part of Macmillan Publishing Group, LLC
175 Fifth Avenue, New York, NY 10010

ANNA AND THE APOCALYPSE. Copyright © 2018 by Blazing Griffin. Based on a screenplay by Alan McDonald and Ryan McHenry. All rights reserved. Printed in the United States of America.

Library of Congress Cataloging-in-Publication Data is available.

ISBN 978-1-250-31880-0 (trade paperback) / ISBN 978-1-250-31881-7 (ebook)

Our books may be purchased in bulk for promotional, educational, or business use. Please contact your local bookseller or the Macmillan Corporate and Premium Sales Department at (800) 221-7945 ext. 5442 or by email at MacmillanSpecialMarkets@macmillan.com.

Book design by Elynn Cohen

Imprint logo designed by Amanda Spielman

First edition, 2018

1 3 5 7 9 10 8 6 4 2

fiercereads.com

Touch not this wee book if you be a thief, or fall out may all yer teeth.
Tear it, harm it with mal intent, among the undead will you torment.
Boil yer hide and rot yer brain, a numpty bampot forever shall you remain.

For Ryan W. McHenry,
The one that started it all

IT WAS TUESDAY.

A regular, boring Tuesday. Really, no different than any other Tuesday that Anna had experienced in her eighteen years on Earth. Wake up, get dressed, get in the car. Her best friend and next-door-neighbor, John, sat beside her in the back seat of her dad's ancient green rust-bucket, eating his daily jam donut for breakfast as they bumped along the same old streets of Little Haven, their Scottish border town, on their way to school. Left at the post office, right at the supermarket, slow down at the zebra crossing, wave to Mrs. Stevens outside the town hall.

Anna sighed, staring out the window at the dull December sky. There had to be more than this out there. *Anything* would be better than another identical day. John raised a silent eyebrow before offering her a bite of his donut. Even his breakfast choice was a stable constant. She declined with a shake of the head as her dad turned the radio up until the car's tinny speakers rattled with the beat. It was all Anna could do to stop herself from opening the door and throwing herself out of the moving vehicle.

The screech of the wheels pulled Anna out of her thoughts as the car came to a sudden stop, her seat belt holding her in place against the force. The same couldn't be said of John's coffee.

"Oh gosh!" cried Anna's dad, Tony, recovering from the emergency stop. In front of them, a lonely figure stumbled out into the street and dropped to the ground. He lay motionless for a moment, and then a pool of blood started spreading slowly from his head.

Well that's a bit different, Anna thought.

✦ ✦ ✦

Thirty minutes later, Anna still had her nose pressed against the window, while John strained against his seat belt, practically sitting himself in her lap. An ambulance flashed its lights silently at the side of the road as someone was being lifted by paramedics onto a stretcher. An arm, clad in a red jacket, fell off the side of the stretcher and swung lifelessly back and forth. The red jacket, the shiny black boots, a very full white beard . . .

"I can't believe Santa's dead!" Anna said sadly.

A long line of traffic had formed behind them up the street, and a crowd of onlookers had gathered to pay their respects as the paramedics pulled up the zipper on Father Christmas's body bag.

Anna watched her dad finish giving his statement to a police officer before heading back to the car.

"That's some poor bugger's Christmas ruined," said her dad, jumping back in and starting the engine.

"Ho ho no," John muttered as Tony pulled out, the traffic following from behind. "Who would *do* such a thing?"

"Easter Bunny," Anna replied with a mischievous smirk. "It's a blatant power move. He's probably in cahoots with the Tooth Fairy—you know she's always been a bad influence."

John shook his head, narrowing his eyes. "That bucktoothed bastard. Who's going to look after the reindeer? And what about the presents?"

"Don't worry, I'm sure Mrs. Claus has it covered. Maybe you can lend a hand . . ." Anna suggested. "You'd make a great elf."

"Who are you calling *elfish*? I'll have you know that

I'm exceedingly generous." He nudged her in the ribs, wiggling his eyebrows up and down.

Anna realized years ago, making bad jokes was as important to John as breathing, and if he wasn't already telling a joke, he was probably thinking about one. At eighteen, she'd given up hope of them ever getting any better. Still, he was the best thing about this town. She didn't know how she would have managed without her BFF over the last few years.

"What have I told you about the puns?" she reminded him in a stern voice that didn't quite cover an attack of the giggles. "While we're on the subject of elves, I reckon your pullover would be quite popular at the North Pole."

John looked down at his ugly Christmas sweater in mock horror.

"You're just jealous because you're not the one dressed like a festive *legend*." He sniffed, proudly pushing out his pigeon chest and thrusting the whole mess in Anna's face.

"Oh God, it's awful," she laughed, pushing him away.

"Wait for it," he replied.

As if the mess of Christmas tree, gaudy baubles, snow, and tinsel weren't enough, John pressed a hidden button and the whole thing lit up, fairy lights flashing on and off.

"You're a lost cause," Anna laughed, pushing him back across the seat with tears in her eyes. "Get off me!"

John bloody *loved* Christmas, but Anna couldn't bear

it. She had loved it as a kid, back when she was all excited about Santa and presents and trying to hide her advent calendar from her mom so she wouldn't find out she'd eaten every chocolate by the fifth of December, but that was before her mom had gotten sick. Before she'd had to say goodbye. These days, on the scale of *Things She'd Really Rather Not Do, Thank You Very Much*, Christmas hovered somewhere in between having her teeth cleaned at the dentist and stabbing herself in the eye with a pencil. She missed her mom a lot . . .

"Anna?"

Something about her dad's tone made it clear it was not the first time he'd said her name.

She gave her dad a forced, cheery smile. She'd gotten good at those.

"Sorry, I was miles away," she said, wishing she really were. *Miles and miles and miles.*

"I said, do you want to pick some music?" he repeated, turning the radio knob. "Any preferences?"

Before Anna could reply, a voice interrupted the static.

"We interrupt your regular program with some sad news," the local DJ announced. "We've just been informed that local Santa, Nathan Ormerod, has sadly passed away—"

Before he could finish, Anna leaned forward between the two front seats and changed the radio station herself.

News in Little Haven traveled fast . . . like, it-happened-two-minutes-ago fast. All across the world, people were living exciting lives, going on daring adventures, and the most dramatic thing to happen in Little Haven was the town boozer, aka Little Haven's Father Christmas, had drunk himself to death after another bender.

"That's sad," Dad commented as Anna and John exchanged a silent look. "I know his mum. I'll send a card."

"At least it wasn't the *real* Santa," Anna said under her breath. "Right, John?"

"Right," he agreed, dramatically wiping the sweat from his brow. "Phew."

"Have you got your ticket for tonight?"

Anna looked up to see her dad grinning at her in the rearview mirror.

"I already told you," she said, pushing her long brown hair behind her ears. "I can't go to the show. I've got to work."

"You deserve a break, love," he said, tapping the steering wheel in time to the music as they rolled along toward the school. "You know what they say about all work and no play."

"Well, I don't need a break," Anna assured him. Not to mention the fact she couldn't afford one.

6

Beside her, John carried on eating his gooey donut, nursing his cup of coffee between his knees, and said nothing. The last thing he wanted was to find himself in the middle of an argument between Anna and her dad. It was December, it was bloody cold, and Tony Shepherd was his lift to school.

And Anna . . . well, Anna was his everything.

"You won't be saying that next year when you're at university—and it's wall-to-wall lectures," Tony told her with a knowing cluck. "What about you, John? Have you heard back from art school yet?"

John shook his head. "Um, no, not yet, Mr. Shepherd."

Tony frowned at him in the mirror. "Is that normal?" he asked.

John gulped hard, accidentally squished the remains of his donut in his hand, curled his shoulders forward, and wished he could disappear.

"Dad!" Anna exclaimed, glancing over at her friend as his cheeks turned bright red. She reached sympathetically toward John's hand but stopped just short.

It was a sore subject. Everyone else knew what they were doing when they finished their exams in the spring but John still hadn't heard back from any of the art schools he'd applied to. Unfortunately, Tony had all the tact of Rudolph after one too many seasonal eggnogs.

"John doesn't need to go to art school anyway," Anna added. "He's already the best cartoonist ever. You ought to be teaching the classes."

"Yeah, wouldn't mind hearing back from at least one school though," he replied, scratching at some jam on the cuff of his sweater. "Be nice to know what I'm doing in September."

Tony offered John an apologetic grin to make up for his gaffe, and John tried to conjure a smile back but just looked as though he had terrible gas.

"I'm sure it'll be fine, son," Tony said. "Hey, why don't you bring Anna to the Christmas show tonight? It's going to be a right laugh."

"I'm working!" Anna reminded her father for what felt like the thousandth time. "And so is he. John, tell him."

"She's working," John mumbled, staring at the remains of his squashed donut, mind still stuck on his missing art school acceptance letter. "She's got to pay off that plane ticket."

"John!" Anna yelped as though she'd been stung.

"What ticket?" Tony asked, confused.

"You said *tell him*," John whispered as his pulse started to beat worryingly fast. All the blood began to drain from his face as he slowly realized what he'd revealed.

"I didn't mean tell him *that*!" Anna replied, wide-eyed.

"What ticket?" her dad repeated.

"It's nothing," Anna insisted. "I'll tell you about it later."

If there was one thing Tony had learned from being a single parent, it was that when your teenage daughter said it was nothing, it was definitely something.

"What ticket, Anna?" he said for a third and final time, breaking out his best stern father voice. Even after all this time, he wasn't very good at it.

"It's just . . ." She searched for the right words to break the news to her dad, but they simply didn't exist. She motioned for a little help from her supposed-best friend, but he turned away, suddenly very interested in something out the window, and about as much use as a chocolate teapot. Out of options, Anna took a deep breath and pasted on a brave smile.

"I'm going on a trip, all right?" she said finally. There, that would do. No more information than necessary. All she had to do was stay calm and they could discuss it later, at home, when she was prepared, and her dad wasn't driving half a ton of heavy metal toward a crowd of her friends. "That's what the ticket is for. No big deal."

"What trip? A school trip?" Tony looked very confused. This was the first he'd heard about any trip.

"No," Anna replied. "Just me. On my own."

"When?" he demanded. "Where?"

Anna bit her lip and looked back out the window.

"Let's talk about it later," she suggested.

"So you can avoid the subject again? I don't think so. We'll talk about it now," Tony countered. "I hope you've checked when university starts, because . . ."

Stay calm, she told herself as her dad started on his well-practiced "The Wonders of College" speech.

"You can't be missing the start of the semester," her dad went on as her blood pressure started to rise. "If you're not there at the beginning, they won't let you start up late, it's not like high school, where you can have a week off here, a week off there, Anna, this is serious grown-up stuff—"

"I'm not going to uni!" she shouted.

Sometimes, staying calm was easier said than done.

Tony slammed his foot on the brakes and the car squealed to a standstill. Anna felt her seat belt snap her back as John's coffee went flying. Dramatic reactions ran in the family. Twisting himself around in his seat, Tony yanked at his own seat belt as he stared at his daughter in disbelief.

"What?" she said innocently, straightening the collar

of her white school shirt. "I don't mean I'm not going ever. I'm going to travel first, that's all. Just for a year, or maybe—"

"Don't be so stupid!" Tony interrupted. "You're doing no such thing."

Anna felt her jaw tighten, defiance written all over her face. She knew her dad would never understand. She knew he wouldn't want to let her go. This was exactly why she had avoided telling him in the first place. She sat silently.

Able to play the same game, Tony started driving again without another word, turned into the school entrance, and pulled into his parking space in the staff parking lot.

"At least no one will notice the jam stain now," John whispered, pulling his coffee-covered sweater away from his body to take a better look at the damage. Anna unclipped her seat belt and jumped out of the car, crossed her arms, and leaned back against the door without a word.

John got out of the car more slowly, trying not to drip the coffee on the seats. "See you inside then," he muttered in Anna's general direction, nervously pulling on the straps of his backpack. "Thanks for the lift, Mr. Shepherd."

Father and daughter gave him exactly the same look as he backed away. Even though Anna would hate him for even thinking it, sometimes she was her dad's double. He was definitely better off out of this one.

"You know this is going to hold you back," Tony said, running his hands through his already messy hair. He was trying so hard not to overreact, but sometimes she made it so difficult. "Where are you planning to go on this trip of yours?"

Anna folded her arms across her chest tighter and shook her head as her friends traipsed past, pretending not to notice them. "Australia first. The ticket's open so I can figure it out as I go."

"Oh, well, that's all right, if it's open, eh?" Tony replied, loading sarcasm into every word. "Think of all the beautiful places you could get mugged or killed!"

"Stop trying to run my life!" she shouted back. "You can't tell me what I can and can't do, I'm not a little girl anymore."

"Then stop acting like one," her dad said loudly, the features on his face pinching together into a picture of disappointment. He shook his head slowly. "If your mother could see you now."

Anna breathed in sharply. Everything around her went quiet. It felt as though he'd punched her in the gut.

"I can't wait to get away from you," she muttered, pushing past her father and heading into school before he could see the massive tears welling in her eyes.

"Anna, wait!"

He wanted to take back the words the moment they were out of his mouth, but it was too late. She disappeared in the crowd, melting into a sea of school uniforms, and leaving him all alone.

2

JOHN HUNG AROUND the school entrance, waiting for Anna to finish talking to her dad. Or rather, fighting with her dad. That was all they seemed to do lately. Still, at least he'd be there to pick up the pieces when they were done.

That's me, he thought to himself. *Reliable old John, always around with a shoulder to cry on.*

Which would have been fine if he hadn't been hopelessly in love with his best friend for at least 1,927 days and counting. If only he could get her to see him in the same way . . . He wandered inside and through the hall, not paying attention to anything that was happening around him. As usual, John couldn't think of anything other than Anna.

"Watch out!"

A piercing shriek broke his daydreams right as he clattered into a full-to-bursting sack of brightly wrapped Christmas presents. Arms flailing wildly, he grabbed at the bag and tried to keep himself upright, but it was too late; the bag exploded and the donated gifts went flying.

"Sorry," John said, dropping to his knees to help pick them up and put them back. "I'm really sorry."

"I got it."

He didn't even need to look up to know who the gifts belonged to; her Canadian accent was a dead giveaway. It was Steph, the school's only international student and resident social justice crusader. John leaped backward out of the way as she grabbed for the presents, a flash of long limbs and platinum-white hair, awkwardly trying to ram them all back into the bag. She moved like she wasn't entirely sure if she was allowed to take up space, and on the rare occasion that she did speak to anyone, she almost always cracked a joke that wasn't quite funny. John never knew what to say to her, so like almost everyone else in the school, he just didn't say much.

"Do you need a hand with these?" he tried.

Anna appeared out of nowhere holding her perfectly wrapped donation and handed it to Steph.

"It's fine," she replied sharply, snatching it out of Anna's hand. "I've got the car, so . . ." She trailed off, gathering the other gifts quickly and running out toward the parking lot.

"I guess we're all having a good day," Anna said, watching as Steph disappeared around the corner. John held his breath until she looked over at him with a weak smile.

"Yeah, right," he breathed out, relieved. She never stayed mad at him for long. "Are you all right? I've never seen your dad that mad before."

Anna nodded. Then shrugged. Then frowned.

"You think I'm doing the right thing, yeah?" she asked, sounding a little unsure of herself. It wasn't a tone John was used to hearing from her.

"Yeah," he said in the least convincing voice ever. "I think it's great."

Anna stared up at him. *Seriously?*

"Anyway." John cleared his throat and flexed his nonexistent bicep. "PE is calling."

Anna waved him off with a sigh and wondered how she had managed to ruin her day so spectacularly before the morning bell had rung. Even for her, that had to be some kind of record.

✦ ✦ ✦

Steph was *also* having a very, very bad day. Veronica, her girlfriend, had flat-out refused to come to visit her for the holidays, and her parents had decided a vacation in Mexico without her was much more appealing than Christmas in Scotland. After all, they were the ones who encouraged her to apply to spend her senior year abroad in the first place. Well, her dad anyway, when he went through their long family lineage from Europe.

She skulked back through the front door, staring at her phone, willing her girlfriend to call back and change her mind.

"Miss North!"

She stopped in her tracks at the sound of his voice. It was Mr. Savage, the assistant principal and quite possibly the most appropriately named one ever. Savage was tall and lanky with faded red hair, uneven, outdated glasses, and a permanent sneer under his thick beard. He was trying very hard not to perspire from his morning patrol of the school's parking lot. If someone told Steph he'd recently arrived on Earth from a far-away alien universe, she wouldn't have questioned it for a second.

"Miss North," he said again, planting himself directly in her path. "I need you to drop the homeless story."

"It's an editorial!" Steph replied. She hated Savage, but she hated injustice even more, and took her role as the editor of the school blog incredibly seriously. Although, to be fair, Steph took everything incredibly seriously. "You can't tell us what we can and can't write about."

"It's a school blog, Miss North, not *The Times*," Savage replied, towering over her. "The city council sets our budgets, so we play nice with the council. Hopefully we get some new computers."

"I'm going to see Principal Gill," Steph said. It wasn't in her nature to give up, even when she probably should. "He's still the head of the school, he can overrule you."

"Be my guest!" Savage declared happily, nodding toward the principal's office. Principal Gill stood outside, proudly displaying his "I'm retiring" badge while accepting farewell gifts from the staff and students.

"He's got two days left," Savage said softly. "And come January, this school, the students, and the blog are mine."

Steph gulped at the very thought.

"Oh, Miss North." He glanced down at the car keys in her hand. "I've told you time and time again."

She gripped the keys tightly. *No. Absolutely no way.*

"Park your vehicle on school property and . . ." He held out his hand. "It becomes school property. Give!"

He yanked the keys out of her grip and his face split with a sickly smile.

"Thank you," Savage said, pocketing the keys before turning his attention to a kissing couple a few steps away.

"Withdraw your tongues!" He continued down the hallway to ruin someone else's day.

Without her car keys, she couldn't deliver the gifts she'd collected for the homeless shelter, and without the blog, she couldn't write the story she'd promised she would. No family, no girlfriend, no presents, and no blog. Steph sighed out loud.

Could today really get any worse?

✦ ✦ ✦

While everyone ran around her, rushing to their first class of the day, Anna lingered by her locker. She had a study period first thing but was in no rush to get to the library. Instead, she stared at a picture stuck to the inside of her locker door. It was a map of Australia. It was her mom's map of Australia.

When Anna was younger, her mom would tell her all kinds of stories about her travels. She'd been everywhere—Cambodia, Peru, Vietnam, Malaysia, New Zealand, South Africa, China, Japan. She'd visited more countries than Anna could even name, but her favorite place of all was Australia. That was where she'd met Anna's dad. It was too hard for Anna to imagine it now, but she'd seen the photos—proof that her dad had been an adventurer himself once upon a time, right up until Anna's mom found out she was pregnant, somewhere between Sydney and Byron Bay.

They came home, they got married, they lived happily, and twelve years later, she got ill and then died. All those adventures were just snuffed out, gone forever. After her mom passed away, Anna and her dad moved to this little town to be closer to her grandparents, but now they were gone, too, and it was just the two of them. She knew he didn't want her to leave, but she had to. She had to see the things her mom had seen, find out what else was in the world. She traced a fingertip along the map, stopping at every place her mom had marked with a star.

Next to the map was a photo of the three of them together, and next to the photo was a postcard, the last thing her mom had sent her. Even though it had a photograph of a gorgeous sunset and a sandy beach on the front, she knew it had been dropped in the mailbox at the local hospital.

"Anna?"

A voice behind her made her jump. She slammed the locker shut to see her friend Chris waving his smartphone in her face.

"Can you check this?" he asked. "It's my show reel for Miss Wright's film class. I'm not sure if it's ready yet, but I'm supposed to present it this morning."

Anna took the phone and smiled. Chris was a sweetheart. For every ounce of bitterness others might have, Chris had twice the amount of innocence and naïveté. She'd watched a ton of his short films and they were usually full of fake blood and guts, sock puppets, and incredibly bad special effects. This one didn't look to be all that different. The bell rang, startling them both.

"Oh no," he whispered as Anna pulled up his film. "I need to pee."

"TMI, Chris," she muttered sweetly, handing the phone back to him.

"I don't have enough time to pee, do I?" he asked, panicking.

"Nope," she replied. "Good luck with your show reel."

"See you at lunch," Chris called back, already running off down the hallway. "Have a good morning."

"Bit late for that," Anna said to herself, opening the locker and pulling out a slim, white, well-worn envelope. She opened it carefully, as though it might fall apart in her hands. Inside was her airline ticket, first stop Sydney, and then who knew where the adventure might take her. She wanted to experience everything; full moon parties in Thailand, Buddhist temples in Tibet, surfing in Nicaragua, that sanctuary for orphaned baby monkeys in Costa Rica that she'd seen on YouTube. Her bucket list was endless, and there was nothing anyone could say or do to convince her that another four years stuck in a classroom was a better option. This was more than a flight voucher. It was her ticket out of there, literally. Out of school, out of Scotland and out of her zombie-like existence. Maybe this life was enough for John and Chris and her dad, but Anna knew she needed more, and now that she had the ticket in her hands, she couldn't wait to get started.

3

THE LITTLE HAVEN High School Christmas Show was an annual town tradition. Every year, the older students signed up to show off their talents, or, more often, lack thereof. Singers, dancers, magicians, and God forbid, one time there had even been a mime. Anna shuddered at the memory as she walked into the hall later that same day, looking for her friend Lisa. Whenever she was feeling trapped or frustrated, Lisa always knew what to say to cheer her up. And if that wasn't enough, she'd been going out with Chris for what seemed like forever. The girl needed to be canonized immediately. Or institutionalized. Anna wasn't sure which.

Anna slid into the back row of chairs and watched as two boys from the grade below attempted a beatbox version of "All I Want for Christmas" on the stage. To say that it was not good would have been the understatement of the year. On the other side of the hall, she noticed a boy from her English class gnawing on his hand while his friend scratched at the noticeboard over and over.

"Stage fright will do terrible things to a person," Anna surmised, settling in to enjoy the awful rehearsals and wait for Lisa. But she didn't have to wait for long. A pretty brunette came running out from backstage, clad in a sexy blue gown that was about as far away from the school uniform as possible. Two costume assistants trailed after her, clutching at the fabric with safety pins hanging out of their mouths as Lisa almost knocked her friend down with an enthusiastic hug.

"What do you think?" she asked, giving a twirl.

Anna looked past her at the scenery on the stage.

"The dress is beautiful," she said. "But it looks like Narnia threw up all over Oz in here."

"I know," Lisa mooned proudly. "Isn't it wonderful?"

It wasn't the word Anna would have chosen to describe it, but she would never squash her closest girl-friend's unbridled optimism. It was, after all, part of what made Lisa, well, Lisa.

"So, I told my dad," Anna said, wincing at the memory of her morning.

"Oh my God." Lisa wrapped her up in a second hug,

and one of the seams of her dress popped open. "Tell me every single little thing."

"Hold still!" ordered the first costume assistant, attempting to pin the dress before Lisa gave everyone in the hall a different kind of show than the one they were expecting.

"Maybe when we're alone?" Anna suggested, nodding to the costume assistants.

"Oh, they're fine," Lisa insisted. "I was sexting Chris earlier and they were helping. It was *hilarious*."

"I'm literally never having sex," the second costume assistant whispered to himself, tears in his eyes.

"So, was it okay?" Lisa asked.

Anna shook her head. Even though she knew she was doing the right thing, she still felt guilty. Her father had spent her entire life trying to be a good dad, and she hated feeling as though she was letting him down.

"Okay-ish?" Lisa asked.

"Not even a little bit," Anna said. "The opposite, in fact."

"Oh, babe." Lisa was all sympathy and cleavage. It was an odd combination.

"Four more cast members called in sick, so we're going to have to change the running order," Savage barked from the auditorium stage. "Please try to remember that hand sanitizer is your friend. Kissing on the mouth is not . . . your friend."

Terrorizing them in the halls simply wasn't enough for him. He'd also appointed himself director of the Christmas show and was just as determined to drain every ounce of fun out of that experience as well. Anna couldn't even begin to imagine what kind of a tyrant he would become once he was actually the principal. She thanked her lucky stars that her days at this school were numbered.

"You two." He pointed at Anna and Lisa. "Why aren't you up on stage? I haven't got all day, I do have other things to do such as run a school."

"I'm not in the show," Anna replied simply. She wasn't afraid of Savage. He was a nasty piece of work but nothing more than a bully; there was nothing he could do to hurt her.

"Oh yes, that's right," he replied with a sickly grin. "Your father is doing my lights."

She stiffened at the mention of her father. He was the school's maintenance man, but he did a bit of everything for everyone. Set up the science labs, made sure the sports equipment was taken care of, looked after the electrics, managed the school football team. He'd even been known to stand in for the home economics teacher once or twice. His pineapple upside-down cake was legendary. Everyone loved Anna's dad. Everyone except Savage.

"When he's finished cleaning the toilets, would you send him my way?" Savage asked, just to be nasty.

"That's not his job!" Anna yelled, losing her temper very quickly.

"Anna," Lisa whispered, trying to catch her friend's hand to calm her down. There was no point; she saw the anger flashing in Anna's eyes and knew it was a losing battle. They'd both be lucky to get away without detention.

But Savage was too pleased with himself to care about one little girl's emotional outburst.

"It will be soon," he said, a distinct threat in his voice. "I think he'd look just smashing with a plunger in one hand and a mop in the other, don't you?"

Anna vibrated with rage as Lisa held her back.

"Now where is my magician?" Savage yelled, his attention already elsewhere. A short, confused-looking teenager stumbled across the stage, tripping over his elaborate black cape. As he fell, he grabbed hold of a rope to steady himself. But the rope was attached to a pulley, and the pulley was attached to a huge star, suspended high above the stage. As soon as the magician let go of the rope, the star hurtled down from the ceiling, headed straight for Mr. Savage.

"Oh bloody hell!"

He leaped out of the way, seconds before it could decapitate him, as Anna and Lisa watched, hands clamped over their mouths. The star swung back and forth on its rope, inches above Savage's head.

"I think it's about time we had a little chat about health and safety." Savage scowled, standing up and ducking the still swinging star. "Everybody up on the stage. NOW!"

Before anyone could do as they were told, the bell rang to signal lunchtime. Two students, dressed in giant plush penguin costumes, began to waddle off toward the cafeteria.

"Get back on stage this minute, you flightless chancers!" Savage ordered. The penguins immediately turned and made for the stage.

"I'll see you after," Lisa whispered, letting go of Anna's hand and dashing toward the stage.

"No, no, no!" gasped the second costume assistant as the dress ripped loudly, from top to bottom. Lisa froze, clutching the fabric together as the star swung back and forth above the reluctant penguins and Savage held his head in his hands.

Anna smiled as she left to go find some lunch. At least the morning hadn't been a complete loss.

Anna strolled down the corridor, smiling at the memory of Savage almost getting decapitated by a falling star. She couldn't wait to tell John. She flicked at the zipper of her jacket, replaying the moment, not paying attention to exactly where she was going when she heard a deep gasping moan directly behind her. Something wasn't right. Anna's adrenaline immediately pumped into her veins, preparing for possible self-defense. She spun around quickly. A bookish girl that she vaguely recognized from the grade below stood inches from her face. Her eyes were glassy and her skin was shiny with sweat. The girl fell forward into Anna.

"Are you okay?" Anna asked.

The girl didn't reply; instead she fumbled for her inhaler, struggling to pop off the cap.

"Do you need me to get help?"

Still no reply. It had to be a pretty bad asthma attack to get her in such a state so quickly. Anna held her up and the girl opened her mouth, as though she wanted to say something but couldn't speak.

"You're going to be okay, just stay here," Anna said, holding out her hands to make sure she understood she wanted her to stay put. "I'm going to get the nurse."

But before she could even try to help, Anna saw something fly past her and hit the girl square in the face. The girl shrieked, dropped her inhaler, and ran off in the other direction. On the floor, right by Anna's foot, was the remains of the missile. It was a gob of mac and cheese. She turned around to see Nick leaning against the radiator, smug smile on his face and a bowl in his hand.

Just when she thought the day was looking up.

"You are such a child," Anna said, zipping up her coat. Anything to put another layer between her and the man-baby.

"A sexy child," Nick replied, only realizing what he'd said after he'd said it. "Wait, no, that's not right."

"Goodbye, Nick," Anna said as she rolled her eyes and strode away down the hallway.

"Hey, come on, don't be like that."

Nick chased after her, running ahead to stop her in her tracks. Anna did her best to look unimpressed. Another person in this town who only ever let her down. But she had to admit, he was cute. A complete and utter idiot, it turned out, but seriously fit. Tall, handsome, with caramel skin and cheekbones that could slice bread. She almost wavered when she stared up into his bright blue eyes.

"Look," he said, fixing her with those very same eyes and gently stroking her arm. "It's almost Christmas, that's when you're supposed to forgive people, yeah? Can't we be friends?"

She took a deep breath in. Maybe they could be friends again. She was sure stranger things had happened, but none that she could think of in that moment. Maybe that sheep they cloned that time.

"And," Nick went on. "If you want to hook up over the holidays, then—"

"Oh God." Anna shoved him out of her way. When would she learn? People did not change.

"Oi, skip off!"

Over her shoulder, Anna heard her dad's voice. Giving her a quick sleazy wink, Nick scarpered in the other direction, leaving them alone. She looked over at her dad, who gave her a tentative smile. If he had any idea what had happened between her and Nick in October, he'd have more to say to him than "Skip off." In fact, Nick would have been lucky if he'd ever be able to skip anywhere, ever again.

"All right?" Tony said.

Shaking her head, Anna turned in the opposite direction. One minute, he was saying what a disappointment she is to him, the next he was attempting to scare away boys on her behalf.

Managing parents was truly an exhausting job.

THE SCHOOL CAFETERIA was like a zoo, only Anna was sure that animals were served better food. She, John, and Lisa sat at their usual table, John wolfing down his lunch while the girls made faces at the questionable cuisine. How were they supposed to eat it when they couldn't even tell what it was? Not that it was stopping John, whose plate was already half empty. One row along and a few tables up, Nick cackled loudly with his idiot friends, but always with one eye on Anna. Even when she turned her back, she could feel him watching her. Because that wasn't too creepy, was it?

"What's that on your face?" Anna asked, pointing at a gray line on John's cheek that hadn't been there that morning.

"Oh, nothing," he replied, balling his hand up inside

the sleeve of his Christmas sweater and rubbing at the mark until his skin was red. Nick had decided he needed a bit of festive decorating in the changing room after PE. "Drew on myself."

"Classic John." Lisa smiled. He smiled back, too embarrassed to tell them the truth. "Savage is losing it. After you left rehearsals, he made Henry Lee cry because he can't break-dance."

"But Henry Lee has a prosthetic," Anna exclaimed.

"Yeah, and he only has one leg," said Lisa.

"What's Savage's deal anyway?" John asked. "Did his parents abandon him to be raised by wolves, or what?"

"I heard he was a twin but both babies got stuck together in the womb and now there's, like, a baby attached to his side and he hides underneath his sweater," Lisa said, leaning across the table with wide eyes. "So now he's the evil twin and the other twin is the good twin, but it's still a baby and it tells him what to do all the time but he just ignores it. Oh, and he's in constant agony."

Anna and John shared a wide-eyed look of concern.

John opened his mouth to correct Lisa but stopped himself. She wasn't the sharpest knife in the drawer, but she was one of the nicest people on Earth, so there wasn't much point in upsetting her.

"I don't think he's got a parasitic twin," Anna said anyway.

"He definitely has," Lisa insisted. "My friend Caroline's sister's cousin's best friend was at school with Savage and he saw it."

"I just thought maybe he got bullied when he was younger or something," John suggested. "Or didn't get what he wanted for Christmas."

"My dad reckons his parents were really strict," Anna said, peeling the foil off her yogurt. "Like, they always thought he was going to be prime minister or something. I guess things didn't work out exactly how he thought they would."

"Things never do," John replied moodily, looking over at Nick and his mates.

"No such thing as a Hollywood ending," Anna concluded right as Chris sat down beside Lisa.

"Disagree!" she exclaimed, grabbing her boyfriend by his collar. "I've got my Hollywood ending already."

Chris barely had time to wave hello to his friends before they launched into their daily lunchtime snogging session. It was almost enough to put even John off his food. Almost.

"How was film class?" Anna asked.

Chris turned his head to answer while Lisa carried on kissing his neck.

"Miss Wright says I need something that shows who I am," he said, as crestfallen as Chris could possibly be.

"I think she liked my *Alien* homage, but she says I need to show her something more real."

"You'll figure it out," Anna said with a supportive smile.

"I hope so," he replied as Lisa moved on to gnawing on his left ear. "I've got no idea what to film. When was the last time anything exciting happened around here?"

Across the cafeteria, Nick and his mates starting laughing even more loudly, and even though they were all trying to pretend he didn't exist, as soon as she heard Nick mention her name, Anna knew exactly what he and his childish friends were laughing about.

"Ignore them," John said stonily. He'd never asked Anna exactly what had happened with her and Nick at his Halloween party because he was perfectly happy not knowing the details. He could cope with her not loving him back, but he couldn't stand it if she started going out with a complete knobhead like Nick.

"He's such a prick," Lisa agreed. "A total idiot. I mean, yeah, he's got a body you could lick chocolate off of, but you'd have to have zero self-respect to even think about . . ."

Anna ducked her head, hiding behind her hair.

"I mean, not you, obviously," Lisa said, attempting to dig herself out of a very deep hole. "I meant all the others!"

Anna's face burned crimson red. John looked crushed.

"Not that there's been loads," Lisa babbled. "You know, it's probably all just rumors. You can't believe everything you hear, can you? I'm sure he hasn't been with that many girls."

"Thanks, Lis," Anna muttered, burying her face in her hands.

Panicking, Lisa let go of Chris's hand for a moment and bundled her friend in a giant hug.

"Love me!" she begged.

As if it were possible not to, Anna thought, laughing as she hugged her back.

"Hey, guys!"

Lisa went back to bothering Chris as Steph appeared at their table. Anna tried to give her a polite smile, while Chris and John just looked outright afraid.

"I need you to film something," she said to Chris. Niceties weren't really something Steph bothered with. It was like she'd heard the stereotype about Canadians being overly polite and decided to prove it wrong.

"Yeah?" Chris didn't care. Chris just wanted to film things. Anything. Once, he'd started following a stray dog with his camera and two hours later, realized he was in the middle of nowhere, completely lost. It had taken them another two hours to find him, and then he'd made them watch his film. And Anna's dad couldn't understand why she was desperate to get away . . .

"Savage keeps screwing with the school blog," Steph explained, hovering nervously next to the table. "So, I want to bypass the school completely and do a video. If we go to the soup kitchen tonight, I can put it out before Christmas and actually show people we have a homeless problem."

"It's the show tonight!" Lisa said, pulling on Chris's sleeve. "And I'm doing a special song about Santa!"

"Miss Wright said in class you need something real," Steph said, not giving up without a fight. "And this is real."

Chris considered it for a moment, gazing into Lisa's sad puppy eyes and then back up at Steph's look of desperation.

"I promise I'll make it back for your song," he said to Lisa. "And my gran will be there as well. She's really excited to see you sing."

"All right." Lisa accepted the compromise with a pout.

"Yeah!" Steph celebrated with a fist pump. "Thank you, this is so cool." She paused and bobbed around on the spot. "Let's see that asshole Savage try to stop this one."

The entire table sat in awkward silence, trying not to giggle.

"Yeah, okay," Steph muttered to herself. "I'll show myself out."

"Oi! Annie Lennox!" Nick yelled the reference to her short platinum hair for the entire cafeteria to hear.

As she turned to leave, Nick hurled a handful of food in her direction, hitting her right in the head. His obnoxious friends burst out into hysterical laughter as Steph picked off the remains and hurried out of the cafeteria, head down and determined not to let anyone see her cry.

"Right," John said, slamming his hands on the dining table. "That's it. I'm going over there."

"Power down your lasers, Iron Man." Anna put her hand on top of his. She didn't want to see him get another black eye.

"He doesn't have lasers," John protested. "They're repulsors."

"Well, Nick doesn't need any more help being repulsive," she replied, watching as Nick wiped his mouth on a napkin, then wiped the used napkin on the face of the boy sitting next to him. He truly was foul. She must have been out of her mind.

"Anyway," she said, turning her attention back to her disgusting lunch. "It's not like you could actually do anything." A fact that was not intended to be hurtful, but it was.

John stabbed the remains of his food with an angry fork while Anna absently stirred her yogurt with a spoon.

"Hey, did you guys hear what happened in science?"

If there was one thing Lisa couldn't stand, it was an uncomfortable silence. Or any silence really.

"Oh my God, Gemma Brand called Miss Hutchie a name and she got all upset and then she got sent outside and . . ."

Anna tuned out Lisa's story. *Let them talk about me*, she thought, noticing she was under Nick's gaze again, and she stared back until he looked away, *let them say whatever they want*. In six months' time, she would be on a plane while the rest of them were still here, chatting on about the latest rumors and gossiping about who shagged who. She was already over it. Just six more months, or according to the countdown app on her phone, 181 days.

If things were different, maybe she'd consider staying, but nothing exciting ever happened and nothing ever, ever changed. She had a feeling that John didn't want her to go, and now she knew that her dad didn't, but it was time for her to strike out on her own. Anna leaned back in her chair, kicked her feet up onto the seat next to her, and gazed out the window as it began to snow. There was such a lot of world to see. She just couldn't imagine a single thing that could possibly change her mind.

✦ ✦ ✦

John had also gotten pretty good at tuning Lisa out over the last seven years. In fact, his selective attention span was probably why they were still such good friends. If only he could select whether or not he was attentive to Anna. But he was in love with her and that was that. Completely and utterly, lie awake at night and imagine the two of them skipping hand in hand through Disneyland, in love with her. But this wasn't Disney, this wasn't a movie where the good guy always gets the girl. This was real life, where your best friend grows up to be super hot and hooks up with a total wanker, while you grow up to be just as awkward as you've ever been and no one even gives you a second glance. He wasn't about to ride in on a white horse and save the princess. He was going to sit there, in his Christmas sweater with permanent marker on his face, and watch the princess disappear halfway across the world.

That was real life.

IT WASN'T AS though Canada was a tropical wonderland, but Steph was so completely over this Scottish winter. She pulled her sleeves down over her fingers and made another attempt at breaking into her own car. It always looked so easy on TV. Maybe she should just give up, confess that she was out of cash, and ask her parents to get her a plane ticket to Mexico, too. What was the point in holding on to her stupid pride if her own girlfriend couldn't even bring herself to spend the holidays with her? If she even was her girlfriend anymore.

"Sure, I'll finish school abroad," she muttered to herself as the whole school emptied out into the parking lot. "Sure, Scotland sounds swell. Who wouldn't want to immerse themselves in their Celtic heritage? Sure, I love the rain and the snow and the miserable weather and the shitty food and the mean kids and sociopathic assistant principal who steals your car keys when all you're trying to do is deliver a bunch of Christmas gifts to homeless children."

A bunch of students wearing ridiculous Christmas-themed hats walked past, saw her trying to bust in to the car, and laughed.

"Really?" she said. "You're wearing a hat shaped like a roast chicken and you're laughing at me?"

But they were already gone.

"Meat is murder!" she yelled.

With an exasperated grunt, Steph gave her tire an almighty kick.

"Fuck!" she howled, pressing her lips together to stop herself from crying. Maybe her car tires were made of stone. "Ow."

"Want me to call someone?" Anna asked, wandering across the parking lot with a helpful smile on her face.

Steph sighed inside. Why was this chick always around when she was making an idiot out of herself? Sure, she was cute and she seemed pretty nice, but Steph had also heard she'd been hooking up with that mega-asshole Nick, so she couldn't be all that smart.

"I tried," she replied. "My girlfriend won't pick up."

"Locksmith?" Anna suggested.

"I have no cash," she admitted. "And my parents are in Mexico, so they aren't going to be any great help."

"I wish I was in Mexico," Anna said, leaning against Steph's car. "Sun, good food, tequila . . ."

"And five thousand miles away from your weird-ass daughter," Steph abruptly interrupted.

Anna smiled and nodded. "Oh, I'd happily move my dad a few miles away from here right now."

"Can you stop talking?" Steph said rather rudely. Anna stood up, more than a little taken aback. "Try being moved to an entirely different continent whether you like it or not."

"I'm sorry," Anna said, coiling her long hair around her hand, suddenly very uncomfortable. She'd only been trying to be nice.

"At least you don't have a mom on your case about every little—" Steph stopped as her brain caught up to her mouth. This was Anna. Anna's mom had died. Could Steph get her foot any farther down her own throat?

"I am so sorry," she said, pushing her own platinum hair out of her face. "I didn't mean that."

Anna nodded, sticking her hands deep inside her pockets, balled up into tight little fists.

"Really, I, uh, I always say the wrong thing," Steph said, an uncomfortable chuckle in her voice. "It's kind of my style. Really, I am sorry. About your mom. And also for what I said. About your mom."

Anna gave her a tight smile and then began to walk away, leaving Steph all alone with her locked car and no way of getting inside.

"Merry Christmas, Stephanie," she mumbled to herself before recommitting to breaking in. "And a very shitty New Year to you."

✦ ✦ ✦

Arthur Savage held open his blinds with his thumb and forefinger and watched the students pour out of the school like rats abandoning a sinking ship. Laughing, joking, enjoying themselves . . . They had no idea what the real world was like, no idea what nightmares they would have to face once they left this school. He'd done his best to prepare them, of course, dedicated his life to making sure they were ready. But did they listen? Of course they didn't, they were children. And children, Savage had discovered during his decades as an educator, were ultimately deeply stupid. Oh yes, people loved to talk about the wonder of childhood, the importance of raising the next generation, but he'd been a teacher for twenty-three years, and every single one of his students had been a disappointment. He had fought and strived and sacrificed but slowly, surely, his will to want more for them had ebbed away. Where were his world leaders? Where were his Nobel Laureates?

"Piss bus drivers maybe," he said, watching as one student ran around in circles with what looked like a chicken on his head.

No, the next generation was doomed. All they cared about were selfies, likes, and retweets. The planet could go to hell in a handbasket and they wouldn't care, as long as their YouTube channel was still getting views. Gill had been too soft on them. Thirty years, that man had been principal. Thirty years! And in all that time the school had done nothing but churn out loser after loser after loser while Savage slogged away, wasting his life on undeserving ingrates. He looked back at his office. The poky, dusty *assistant* principal's office. If he could just hang on for two more weeks, then he'd finally be in charge. Then things would change around here.

"I believe the children are our future," Savage sang menacingly, turning back to the window and observing the children as they jumped on one another's backs, pelted one another with foodstuffs, and generally behaved like animals. "And if that's the case, God help us all."

He let the slats of his blinds snap back into place, just as someone knocked on his locked door.

"Who is it?" he bellowed, straightening his tie. Clothes maketh the man, after all.

"All right there, Arthur?"

As if to prove his point, he opened the door to Tony Shepherd.

He returned to his position behind his desk. Maintaining professional distance helped Shepherd grasp that Savage had authority over him. Savage wasn't one to invite someone to sit on a comfy sofa, or offer a jar of sweets.

"I prefer Mr. Savage when we're in school," he said, the edges of his lips curling up at the state of the man. "And outside of school."

"So everywhere then?" Tony replied with a laugh.

Savage did not laugh, but if Tony was offended, he didn't show it. What he did show was dirt under his fingernails, filthy marks on his knees, and, if the assistant principal wasn't very much mistaken, tomato sauce stains on his shirt.

"I'm going to nip home for some tea before the show, but I'll be back here for six o'clock," Tony said, shoving his hands into his trouser pockets. "It's a hungry business, this show business!"

"Like no business I know," Savage replied in a droll voice. The sight of Tony's unshaven face was enough to kill his own appetite. "Is that all?"

"I was thinking," Tony began, but Arthur could barely

believe it was true. "Have you got any plans for the Christmas break?"

"Oh yes," he replied with a wide smile. "I've got plans."

So many plans. Plans to turn this idiot factory into something approximating a school as soon as his name was above the front door.

"I was thinking, why don't you come over for dinner on Christmas Eve?" Tony suggested. "Doesn't do to be on your own at this time of year, Arthur."

Savage glared at him from behind his desk.

"Mr. Savage," Tony corrected with a soft chuckle. "We'll be cooking up a feast, lots of food to go around."

"We?" Savage replied. "You mean you and your interminable offspring?"

"Well, I usually call her Anna." Tony nodded. "It's shorter."

"And you want me to come to your house and eat a meal with you?" He could barely believe what he was hearing. Tony and Arthur were not friends. They had never been friends, they would never be friends. He must want something from him; Arthur firmly believed no one in this world did anything out of the goodness of their own heart anymore.

"Yes, Arthur," Tony said, clearly incapable of following even a simple instruction. "I am inviting you around

to our house for dinner on Christmas Eve. It'll be fun."
Neither of them looked convinced by this statement.
"And maybe you can talk some sense into Anna. Seems
she's decided to go traveling rather than bother with university, and God knows she isn't going to listen to her
old dad."

And there it was.

"Is that so?" Savage wasn't surprised. "She's a bright
enough girl."

"Gets that from her mum." Tony smiled, a wistful
tear in his misty eyes.

Arthur wasn't quite finished. "She's also rude, ignorant, and has absolutely zero respect for authority."

"Aye, gets more of that from me, I reckon," he
replied. "Proud and free spirited like her mother, but
stubborn like her old dad. What a combo. She's just a
dreamer."

"She's a lost cause," Savage countered.

"I don't know about that." Tony very nearly looked
ever so slightly upset. "Anyway, can we expect you
Thursday evening?"

Savage stared at the fat, scruffy, middle-aged man.

"No," he said, astonished. "Absolutely not."

"Right you are," Tony relented. "See you at six."

"Five thirty," Savage barked as Tony saw himself out.

It wasn't just the children who needed to learn to do as they were told.

"They'll learn," Savage said quietly, his eyes following Tony out of the building, across the parking lot, all the way back to his wreck of a car. "One way or another, they'll all learn."

"I REALLY WANT you to get under the skin of this place," Steph explained, pulling the sleeve of her sweater down over her hands to open the door to the soup kitchen. It was freezing outside. "Lots of close-ups, lots of expressions. Who are these people? Where have they been? How did they end up here?"

"I don't know," Chris replied. "How *did* they end up here?"

Steph sucked in her cheeks and exhaled slowly.

"I wasn't asking you to answer the question yourself," she said slowly. "What I meant was, that's what we're here to find out. We're investigative reporters, we're documentarians. We're going to answer the difficult questions that society would rather ignore."

"Right." Chris nodded, the tip of his tongue sticking

out the corner of his mouth. "Like, what's going on with Kanye or is the dress blue or is it white? Lisa thought it was gold but I was like, Lis, that's not even an option . . ."

"Just, no," Steph interrupted. They hadn't even started yet, and she was totally ready to gag him. "Follow me and point the camera where I tell you to, okay?"

"Okay, boss," he confirmed with a thumbs-up and a goofy grin.

"And think more Michael Moore than Michael Bay," she said as they walked inside. "If there's an explosion here tonight, something has gone very wrong."

"Oh, don't worry." Chris whispered as they walked inside. "I can always add them in afterward. I'm a special effects boss."

"Yeah, whatever," Steph groaned, silently reminding herself it was better to have Chris the cameraman than no cameraman at all. She had to get this story. It was important and being ignored, and no one was prepared to tell it but her. Plus it would really stick it to Savage and the council, but most importantly, it would totally help the homeless community. She cleared her throat and concentrated on the task at hand.

"Hello!" Chris stepped in front of her and stuck his hand out toward the tall, bearded man walking toward them. "Can you tell us who you are, where you've been, and how you ended up homeless?"

"Chris!" Steph gasped as the man shook Chris's proffered hand, a look of confusion on his face. "This is Mr. McKnight, he runs the soup kitchen!"

"So, he's not homeless?" he asked, still shaking Mr. McKnight's hand and looking him up and down. The man looked down at him with a tight smile.

"No," she replied, wishing the ground would open up and swallow her whole. "Mr. McKnight, I am so sorry."

"Not at all," he replied, although she could see him turning pink under his black beard. "I take it you've never been to a soup kitchen before, lad?"

"No," Chris said, shaking his head and still wondering why an adult like Mr. McKnight would be wearing those terrible shoes if he had a choice in the matter. "First time. Soup kitchen virgin."

"We're here to educate as much as to assist. I'm sure you'll leave here tonight with a better understanding of what we do," Mr. McKnight said, standing back so Chris could see the entire place. It was much bigger than Chris thought it would be, and it didn't look anything like a kitchen. In fact, it looked fairly depressing. Rows of tables and mismatched chairs filled the space, while fluorescent lights flickered on and off overhead, casting yellow shadows on defeated faces. "We're so glad you wanted to do this, Stephanie. It'll really help us out."

"Just Steph is fine," she replied, smiling politely. "I'm

thinking we start by getting some B-roll footage and then maybe chat with one or two of your . . . guests?"

Mr. McKnight nodded. "Aye, I've got a couple of regulars who are happy to talk with you. And some of the volunteers, too, if you're interested in talking to them."

"That would be awesome," she agreed as Chris turned his camera on and started to record. A few people sat by themselves, keeping to the corners of the tables with their steaming bowls of soup, while others sat in groups, laughing and forcing smiles. On the opposite side of the room, an entire family sat together, kids tucking in happily while Mom and Dad exchanged heavy glares across the table.

"And I'll need to get a few words from you at the end," Steph said, checking her notes on her phone. "Then we'll clear out."

"You're very welcome to stay," Mr. McKnight offered. "We have more than enough to go around tonight. People tend to be more generous at this time of year. It's January and February when times get tough."

"Thanks, but I've got to go and see my girlfriend in the school play," Chris said, still filming. "She's doing a special song, it's going to be epic."

"I'd love to stay," Steph replied. She had nowhere else to be. "Maybe I can help with the cleanup?"

"Fantastic." Mr. McKnight clapped his hands together,

and Chris almost dropped his camera. "I'll let you get what you need and you'll come and find me when you're done, aye? Thank you again."

Chris gave the man a wave as he walked away, disappearing through a little swinging door that flapped back and forth to reveal the actual kitchen. It looked like the school kitchen. In fact, it smelled like the school kitchen. *No wonder I don't like this place*, he thought to himself. Nothing more depressing than school lunches.

"God, this is quite depressing," Steph said, savoring the misery. This was going to be the best video ever, she was going to get so many hits. Not that it mattered how many hits she got, not that she cared. Except maybe, just a little.

"That's just what I was thinking!" Chris exclaimed. "Steph, can you read minds?"

"Generally speaking, no," she replied. "But I've got a feeling yours might not be that difficult to crack. Let's get some background footage."

"What made you want to be an investigative reporter?" Chris asked, guiding his camera around the room, zooming in on the Christmas tree that sat in the corner as Steph removed a couple of baubles to make it look a little more sad. "Are your parents journos?"

"My dad is an investment banker and my mom is . . ." She paused as she pulled a wing off an angel. "My mom."

"Must have been nice to have a stay-at-home mom," Chris commented, turning his camera onto Steph's face. Judging from her expression, he'd said the wrong thing.

"Maybe it would have been if she'd ever stayed home," she replied. "Or if she had interest at all in actually being a mom. Who wants to hang out with your kid when you could be at yoga, right?"

He pulled out on the shot as Steph pointed over at a group of volunteers walking in the front door with heavy sacks of potatoes. "I got really lucky with my gran, she's basically the best ever."

"Your gran?" She had to admit, she'd never thought about his family before. He was always so busy sticking his tongue down his girlfriend's throat, she pretty much tried to avoid the pair of them as much as possible. "What about your folks?"

"My mom died when I was a baby and my dad left right after she died," Chris said with a little shrug. "Couldn't cope with me on his own."

Steph felt a massive wave of regret wash over her. Her sarcasm melted away.

"I'm so sorry," she said, rocking backward onto her heels. "That sounds, ah, really tough."

"My gran always says we each have our own cross to bear," he recited. "But I don't think I'm missing out on too much. She's awesome, my gran."

"Maybe we should trade," she joked, slowly replacing the baubles on the tree under the watchful eye of a particularly judgmental little girl.

"I would like to go to America," Chris replied, clearly considering it.

Steph narrowed her eyes into tiny slits.

"I'm not American. I'm Canadian."

"Really?" He stared back at her with wide eyes.

"Really." She rolled her eyes back so far, she was sure she could see the edge of her brain.

"I love Drake," Chris said, still beaming at this exciting piece of news. He'd never met a Canadian before. But then he realized that meant he'd never met an American, and the smile slipped off his face.

"They film loads of stuff in Canada these days," he said, attempting to cheer himself up with movie trivia. "Like all the X-Men movies. It's supposed to be set in New York but they filmed it in Toronto. Me and John looked it up and—"

"Yeah, Canada is kind of boring," she cut him off and abruptly stood up. "I'd rather not talk about it."

"Is that why you left?" Chris asked.

"I left because my high school was offering an international travel exchange and I thought they were going to send me to Paris," she replied, exasperated. "But hey, tiny town on the Scottish border, practically the same thing, right?"

"Oh no," he replied. "I've been to Paris. We went on a school trip in year nine and John was sick on the coach and Anna dared me to eat frogs' legs and honest, Steph, it's nothing like Little Haven."

"Oh, sweet baby Jesus, give me strength," she said, turning her eyes skyward and praying to a God she had made it quite clear that she didn't believe in, at her cousin's Catholic wedding. "Okay," she said, clapping her hands and giving Chris a dazzling smile. "Shall we get on with the interviews so you can get back to your girlfriend?"

"Lisa said you've got a girlfriend," Chris said, following her back across the room.

Steph stiffened. Great, they were talking about her now. Didn't want to talk to her or hang out with her or invite her to their parties but at least she was good for some locker-room gossip.

"Is she in Canada?"

"Yes."

"Do you miss her?"

"Yes."

"I can't imagine how I would feel if Lisa went to live in another country," Chris said with a lovesick sigh. They both jumped as one of the volunteers suddenly burst out in a coughing fit. Steph grabbed the lens of Chris's camera and pointed it in his direction without a moment's hesitation. "I think me and Gran would have to move there with her. But then we'd have to leave Little Haven and I don't really want to do that."

"And if Lisa was a guy, your gran might not be so supportive of your relationship," she muttered back under her breath. "Perhaps she'd practically pack your bags for you. Adios, awkward gay child I don't want to discuss at brunch."

"Oh no," Chris replied as the coughing man recovered himself and sipped a glass of water, still shaking. "She's fine with all that. Gay, straight, bi, queer, trans. Gran watches a *lot* of YouTube."

"Maybe we *should* trade," Steph said as Chris chuckled and carried on filming. *There has to be something wrong with this kid*, she thought to herself as he slowly panned around the room. No mom, abandoned by his dad, and stuck in this dead-end town with no desire to leave. What did he know that she didn't? His face was all scrunched up as he stared at the screen of his camera, panning slowly around the room.

"Hey, Chris," Steph said, concentrating on straightening her tie as she spoke. "What is it you love so much about this town anyway?"

He looked at her with genuine confusion. *How could she not see it?*

"Everything?"

"Wow," Steph replied with a whistle. "Whatever you're on, can you get me some?"

"I did smoke weed once but it made me really hungry and I tried to make scrambled eggs with chocolate but I kept getting all the shell in it and then I got upset and I had to eat seven bags of cheesy puffs and then I had to sleep behind the sofa in case a monster unicorn came to get me." He took a deep breath and shook his head. "Haven't touched it since."

"Right. Let's just shoot the video," she said, rubbing a hand over her forehead.

"You didn't answer my question," Chris said, focusing in on the volunteers ladling out bowls of steaming hot soup. "Why are you so into all this stuff? The investigative reporting stuff? The movies I make are loads more fun."

"I think the world needs to know these things are happening," she replied, her voice light, as though she was afraid the words might crack and break. "And I want to share people's stories, I want to give a voice to the voiceless."

"It's funny you're into all this stuff when you don't really have many friends." When she didn't reply, he turned to look at Steph and winced at the expression on her face. "Sorry," he said, genuine anguish on his face. "I didn't mean it like that. Only that you're usually hanging around on your own at school and stuff. You've probably got friends outside school."

"No, you're right," she said with an awkward laugh. "I don't really have any friends here. Or at home. Or anywhere."

"You've got your girlfriend, though," Chris said encouragingly.

Steph wrinkled up her nose. "I guess."

"And you've got your blog," he added.

"Yeah, people on the internet are a lot more reliable than people I-R-L," she said, watching as a larger woman smashed in through the front door, wobbling as she walked. Someone had already been on the eggnog. "Mostly reliable assholes, but still. Consistency is key."

"That's the spirit," he said, slapping her roughly on the back and making her cough. "My gran always says everyone has a good side, even if you can't see it."

"Even her?"

She nodded toward the newest arrival, right as she walked straight into a wall and doubled over to puke in a trash can.

"It takes all sorts, Steph," Chris said with unearned

wisdom as Steph tried to repress her own gag reflex. "It takes all sorts."

"Let's just get this over with," she said, holding her forearm in front of her face. "You need to leave and I need to . . . leave."

"I hope we don't get sick," Chris said as another table of people all started coughing. "Seems like there's something going around. I don't want to be ill for Christmas."

"Probably something they picked up on the streets," Steph replied, glad she'd taken her immunity booster that morning. "It must be so hard for them . . . Let's make sure we get lots of footage of the people coughing, okay?"

"You're the boss," Chris said again, heading into the fray with his camera.

"This is going to be the best vlog ever," Steph whispered gleefully.

Tony was right, Anna had always been a dreamer.

When she was a little girl, she had wanted to be a writer. In the bottom of her wardrobe were boxes and boxes of half-finished stories she'd written before she decided writing took too long and she needed something more immediate. That was when she decided she wanted to be a photographer and never went anywhere without her mom's camera. When she couldn't capture the images she felt in her heart, she turned her hand to painting. And then sculpting. She'd also been through her musician phase, her sports phase, and her science phase, but never, even in her wildest dreams, could she have imagined the one thing she'd stick at for more than six months, would be this.

Thunderballs.

She'd been working part-time at the local bowling alley ever since she turned sixteen, and even though it was literally the most part-time job that had ever existed, she was determined to stick it out. Maybe she'd given up on the guitar before she got past three chords, and perhaps she wasn't going to be winning the Nobel Prize for Literature anytime soon, but for every hour she spent handling sweaty, two-toned shoes in a darkened bowling alley full of creeps, she was five pounds and ninety pence closer to achieving her ultimate dream.

The parking lot was full when she arrived and she felt her shoulders drop. It was bound to be busy this close to Christmas. There weren't many options for Christmas parties in Little Haven. It was basically Pizza Hut, the Harvester, or Thunderballs, and you couldn't sneak your own bottles of Mad Dog 20/20 into Pizza Hut or the Harvester. At least not without being really stealth.

Her nose burned from the cold as she trod carefully through the snowy parking lot, steeling herself for another long, uneventful evening.

A random man emerged from the shadows and walked right into her. He kept going as she recovered herself, unsteady on his feet, and it seemed not entirely sure where he was going.

"Sorry!" Anna said automatically, even though it was

clearly the man who wasn't looking where he was going. He turned, his face hidden in shadows, and slowly began to zigzag toward her.

"Someone started early," she muttered under her breath before checking her watch. She was already late. No time to give him a lesson in manners.

And so Anna didn't see the blank look in the man's eyes, the bite mark on his hand, or the blood running down his chin. If she had, she might have been better prepared for what happened next.

✦ ✦ ✦

By the time Anna arrived, John had already mopped the café floor, polished all the bowling balls, and managed to consume two packets of crisps from the stockroom. He'd also clocked Anna in on time, just like he always did. He didn't mind working at the bowling alley. It was a lot better than working in Little Haven's one-screen cinema, like Chris. That boy always smelled like a fresh bucket of popcorn, and at the bowling alley, John was a lot less likely to end up getting his hand buttered and burned. That said, it had been a particularly trying evening at Thunderballs. They'd been swarmed with Christmas parties, all ten lanes occupied all night long, and the last few would not leave. He saluted Mrs. Hinzmann, the cleaner who ignored him as usual, and wandered over to the shoe counter to find his friend.

"Oh!" he exclaimed, reeling from the overpowering stench of sweaty feet. "You smell like a shoe."

Anna spritzed her giant can of shoe-deodorizing spray in his general direction. She'd gone nose blind to it a long time ago; it was one of her superpowers now. Over on lane ten, a group of rowdy men from the garage down the road, draped in tinsel and plastic reindeer antlers, cheered for another strike. A combined Christmas party and bachelor night. The worst possible combination of parties in human history. They'd been there for hours, and showed no sign of tiring. Any other Tuesday, she'd have been home by now, tucked up in bed, planning her travels, but parties like this dragged on forever.

"Christmas is fast becoming my least favorite C-word," Anna said, spraying down another pair of shoes.

"You wouldn't be saying that if you were dressed like a festive legend!"

John struck a dramatic pose, and the lights of his Christmas sweater began to dance in time to the terrible music that played over the speaker.

"You're right," Anna agreed, pressing her forefingers to her temple and pretending to shoot herself in the head. She couldn't believe he was still wearing that thing.

"Although dressed like that, you know you look like a massive C-word, right?"

"Grinch," John replied. He rested his elbows on the counter. "Bit gutted to be missing the Christmas show tonight. Graham and Sunil have turned 'Frosty the Snowman' into a freestyle rap. I heard them rehearsing in biology. It's pretty good. Very Jay-Z meets Kanye."

"Shouldn't they have been doing biology in biology?"

The men from the garage bowled their last frame, and Anna immediately grabbed their shoes and lined them up on the counter.

"This close to the holidays, who cares?" John sniffed, trying not to stare at his friend. She was just so pretty. And funny. And clever. And now he was definitely staring. "Mr. Evans was reading comics all through class anyway."

"Sounds about right," Anna said, clapping loudly to try to get the bachelor party's attention. "Good game, guys, but we're closing now. Come get your shoes."

They all stumbled over in one large group, all taller, bigger, and beefier than John. He hovered at the edge of the crowd as they threw their bowling shoes at Anna and grabbed their own footwear from the counter. The rank smell of feet blended with cheap alcohol and stale cigarettes to create a perfume that could only be found in bowling alleys worldwide. *There should be a support group,* he thought. Just a whiff of that, wherever he was in the world, and he'd immediately feel compelled to start mopping up vomit.

"Animals," he muttered. This was why he needed to get into art school: He wasn't one of them. It was like Anna always said, they were different. She said John had an artist's soul, and he liked that. He didn't love it when she said he was a sentimental softy, but he knew she was only joking. Most of the time.

Anna ushered the tinsel-sporting men out the front door. The tallest of the bunch held out his arms, as if to give her an unwanted hug, but at the last second, he staggered forward and tripped over his own feet. Anna panicked and leaped out the way, clapping a hand over her mouth as he landed in a heap on the floor.

"I'm okay," he said, grinning as his friend dragged him out into the cold night air. "That's going to hurt in the morning."

"On Dasher, on Dancer," Anna said, pushing the last stragglers out into the cold. "On . . . other ones?" She locked the door tightly and waved to the men, still staring blankly at one another in the snow.

"Firebolt?" John suggested. "No, that's Harry Potter's broom, isn't it?"

"Oh no!" Anna exclaimed, turning quickly and pressing her back against the door.

"What?" John asked, immediately panicking.

Anna dropped a heavy hand on his shoulder.

"We can't hang out anymore," she declared gravely. "I'm afraid you're too sad."

"Look, it's a very popular series of books," he said, his face flushing red as he followed Anna back to the shoe counter. "And everyone has read them."

"Peak sad!" Anna laughed. "Sorry, John."

"Ahem."

Mrs. Hinzmann, always lurking around a corner with her broom, cleared her throat and gestured for the two of them to look at the floor. One of the pairs of bowling shoes that Anna had been cleaning were on the floor, right by her bucket.

"Sorry, Mrs. Hinzmann," Anna said, dashing across to pick them up. Sure, she looked like your average, quiet old lady, but you did not want to get on the wrong side of Mrs. Hinzmann. Anna couldn't prove it, but she was almost certain that she was the one who had put a moldy tuna sandwich in her gym bag earlier in the summer, after Anna had accidentally knocked over a bucketful of dirty water on the lanes. The older woman pointed toward her eyes and then pointed at Anna, sending chills down her spine, before disappearing into the staff room. Anna picked up the broom from the cleaning cart, raised it above her head, and struck one of the bowling shoes.

"Hole in one!" she yelled as the shoe sailed through the air, over the counter, and landed, with a thud, in the bottom of the bin.

"All right, whatever," John said, brushing imaginary dust off his shoulders. "Watch this."

He picked up the other shoe, placed a hand over his eyes, and prepared to toss it with all his might right as Mrs. Hinzmann reemerged from the staff room.

"John, wait!" Anna yelled.

John did not wait. He threw the shoe like he was throwing a dart at a bull's-eye and it flew right into the back of Mrs. Hinzmann's head, knocking her over.

The pair of them froze, eyes glued to the motionless old woman, laid out unconscious on the floor. Anna looked up at John. John looked back at Anna. Mrs. Hinzmann still didn't move.

"Oh my God," gasped John. "I've killed Mrs. Hinzmann."

8

BACK AT SCHOOL, the Christmas show was not going well. Not as bad as accidentally killing a cleaning lady, but still, not great. Savage and Anna's dad sat in the lighting and control booth in the back of the auditorium facing the stage as two students dressed as rapping penguins walked out to light applause. Showtime. Tony cued the music while Savage studied his approved lyrics sheet. Every participant had been required to submit all details of their performance, in writing, to be screened in advance. The last thing Little Haven needed was a repeat of The Great Accidental F-Bomb of 2012.

> *My favorite dish is fish, mother flipper,*
> *And I eat it for the hell of it,*
> *A nice bit of halibut.*

That's not the only fish they've got,
Mackerel (mackerel).
I can take more than a snack full,
Salmon with some jam on.
I could drink it by the tap full
Haddock's always radical,
I eat the fins, I eat the gills.
Pollock, cod, flounder, guppy,
All fish is delicious to me.

Unfortunately, reading along with the lyrics did not make them better.

"They're a laugh," Tony said, reaching out to turn up the music.

"They're abominable," Savage corrected, slapping his hand away from the knob. "Four weeks of lunchtime rehearsals and for what?"

"At least they're trying," Tony commented.

"Very," Savage agreed, closing his eyes and pressing his fingertips into his temples as the chorus hit.

There's plenty of fish in the sea, baby,
But there's not enough fish for me (yo, fish is delish).
We say there's plenty of fish in the sea, baby,
But there's not enough fish for me.

After what felt like forever, the penguins wrapped up, and the audience clapped weakly. So far they'd had the world's worst rapping penguins, three boys in leotards dancing to Beyoncé's "Single Ladies," and a girl who vomited on stage halfway through her reimagining of *A Christmas Carol*, set in a dystopian future, run by robots.

"This is the worst show yet," Savage announced. If the eyebrows on the senior girls hadn't already sealed it, he was now utterly convinced that this generation would be responsible for the end of all things.

"Ahh, you know they mean well, Arthur," Tony said, clapping him on the back. Savage almost choked on his own tongue. "Phil was telling me about these lads last night."

"Phil?" Savage repeated. "You mean Mr. Evans?"

"Yeah, that's right," Tony said. The penguins shuffled off the stage, bumping into each other as they went. "We were talking about the show over Christmas cocktails last night."

Savage squeezed his jaw so tightly, it was a wonder his teeth didn't shatter. He hadn't been invited to any Christmas drinks. Not that he would have gone, but still. Was there any wonder the children had no respect for him when the teachers couldn't even attempt to show any?

"Anyway, I was telling Phil, it's nice of you to help the children out like this, Arthur." Tony rested a hand on his forearm, just for a second. The look on Savage's face made it quite clear the gesture wasn't welcome. "A lot of these kids are going through difficult stuff," Tony went on, crossing his arms across his chest and nestling his hands underneath his armpits. "This show gives them something to focus on. I know you don't want people to know it, but underneath it all you're a good man, Mr. Savage."

"I can assure you I am not," Savage said in his soft, ominous voice. "A good man does not make a great educator. We can't trust these idiots to do anything by themselves, Tony. If I let them run this show without close supervision, it would be chaos. Obscene chaos. They're no better than animals."

"They're children," Tony argued. "You could go a bit easier on them."

Savage turned to give him the full weight of his sneer. No wonder his daughter behaved the way she did. No wonder she thought she could run off around the world and have her life waiting for her on a plate when she got back. They might not realize it, but they needed someone like him, he realized as the next act took the stage, now more than ever. Shepherd was wrong. He needed to be harder on them, not easier. They needed firm discipline, a strong leader, someone who knew right from wrong.

"Hit it!"

Tony hit a button, triggering a fake snowfall, and a spotlight lit up the stage, illuminating Lisa in her sparkly blue sequins. The orchestra struck up a sexy jazz beat, and Lisa turned around to reveal a very different dress from the one Savage had approved. She elegantly wiped a rogue snowflake off her eyelashes, leaned forward toward the microphone, and smiled.

"There's a lack of presents in my stocking, and my chimney needs a good unblocking," she crooned as four shirtless male dancers appeared on each side of her, wearing nothing but tight red-and-white flocked shorts, knee-high socks, and green elf hats.

"These are not the approved lyrics," Savage breathed. "This is not what we rehearsed."

"If you're feeling frozen stiff, my fire's burning hot for you," Lisa sang, tiptoeing around her dancers while the audience stared, equal parts horrified and delighted. It was enough to make Miley Cyrus blush. *"Before you take a nap, let me sit upon your lap, there's only one gift that I wanna unwrap. Baby, it's that time of year!"*

"Mr. Gill seems to be enjoying it," Tony said, coughing uncomfortably.

Mr. Gill clapped along happily in the front row while Chris's gran gave her two thumbs up, both of them blissfully ignorant to the meaning of Lisa's lyrics. Along the same row, a horrified mother slid her hand subtly over her toddler's eyes while one of the recently single-again divorced dads whistled a catcall, loudly.

"Gill is an imbecile," Savage declared. "I'm going to kill her. Turn off the lights."

"You can't do that," Tony argued, even though he was unsure where to look himself. He'd watched little Lisa run around his back garden when she was a toddler. How was it possible that she was now giving a teenager dressed as a Santa stripper a lap dance in front of the entire town?

"I'm going to get some fresh air," Savage replied, pushing his chair away angrily and abandoning the booth. "This show is a disaster."

"Come on, Santa!" Lisa sang, thrusting one arm up in the air as she realized Chris's seat was still empty. She tried hard to not show her disappointment. He hadn't made it back in time for her song after all. *"Give it to me!"*

The whole hall burst into thunderous applause as she finished the song, but she could only see Chris's empty seat. Forcing a smile, she took a bow with her dancers. Where could he have been that was more important than her show? Heartbroken, she slipped off the stage, still smiling for her adoring fans, and went in search of her phone.

✦ ✦ ✦

Outside the hall, Savage closed his eyes and attempted to compose himself. The show was a shambles, and now it was obscene to boot.

"Calm down, Arthur," he said out loud. "In two weeks, you can expel her and then we'll see who's laughing."

At the other end of the corridor, the alarmed fire doors rattled from the outside.

"Who's there?" he called.

He'd given Tony very clear instructions, all doors were to remain alarmed and locked from the inside during the show. He wasn't having the reprobates of this town entering his school, unchecked.

No one replied.

"She'll be the first to be expelled and he'll be the first to be fired," he announced to himself, licking his lips at the very thought as he made his way down the hall to confirm Tony Shepherd's latest failure.

Another bang at the double doors made him jump.

"Why don't they listen to me?" he growled, hitting himself in the head with the heel of his hand. "Why don't they listen to me?"

The doors rattled again.

"Enough!" Savage screamed, panting for breath as the rattling stopped.

Careful not to push the release bar that would set off

the alarm, he gave it a slight tug. Well, there were a million other reasons he could find to sack the man. Before he turned away, Savage thought he saw something move through the narrow slit between the doors. Cold air rushed in through the crack, perhaps an eighth of an inch wide, and he pushed his face right up against the door, desperate to see who was outside.

"Who is out there?" he murmured as what looked like dozens of shadowy figures approached. He fumbled in his pocket for the school keys. If they didn't want to tell him their names, he'd go out there himself and give them what for.

"It's about time the people of this town start listening to me," he declared, holding the tiny silvery key aloft. "Starting with you, whoever you might be."

And then Savage disarmed the doors to the army outside the school walls.

✦ ✦ ✦

"I can't believe you did it," Anna said, biting her lip as she stared accusingly at John. "You little old lady beater."

"Shut up!" he replied, trying to sound threatening. It didn't work. "I mean it, Anna."

"I'm sorry! I'm so, so sorry!" she laughed, unable to keep a straight face for a second longer. She continued to mimic, "Don't move, Mrs. Hinzmann. I'll get you some ice, Mrs. Hinzmann."

"I thought she was dead!" John wailed as Anna ran off into the public playground. They were halfway home, and John was still recovering from the heart attack he'd given himself when he clocked the cleaner in the head with a bowling shoe. It turned out she wasn't dead, but she was very, very unhappy with John.

"I'm so going to lose my job," he sulked, spinning the merry-go-round with one hand. Anna looked up at the falling snow. It was a beautiful night, and for the first time that year, she was starting to feel a little Christmassy.

"I know what'll cheer you up," she said, sitting down in a big patch of untouched snow.

"What, assaulting a cleaner?" John suggested moodily. "Because it wasn't what I hoped it would be, to be honest."

Anna was still laughing as she lay backward, stretching out her arms and legs to make a snow angel.

"And you say I'm the soft one," John said, clambering down into the snow beside her. He flapped his arms and legs wildly. "Oh no, mine's all crap now."

"Yours is brilliant," Anna assured him, even though his angel was crap and he most definitely was the soft one. "Me and Dad used to have competitions every winter when we came up to visit my nan and granddad. Mum would judge to see who could make the best ones but she always let me win."

John reached out his arm until the tips of her fingers were just a snowflake away from his.

"We stopped doing it after she died," Anna said quietly. Without a sound, she took his hand in hers. The friends in the snow, looking up at the sky. The clouds had cleared away, leaving a deep, endless darkness, speckled with pinpricks of starlight.

"John?"

"Anna?"

"What if Dad's right?" she asked, breathing out as she confessed her concerns. "What if I'm just screwing everything up by going traveling?"

"You're Anna Shepherd," he said, turning his head to face her so that his cheek rested in the cold snow. "We both know you're going to end up having some stupidly successful life. It doesn't matter how you do it."

He grinned at his friend and squeezed her hand.

"Big Tony doesn't need to worry about you out there on your own," he promised. "Besides, you won't be on your own for long. I'll come and visit you. We can hike across the outback together."

"That's a pretty long hike," Anna said, giggling, suddenly sure of her decision again. "Are you sure you're up to it?"

"I'll start running to school," he reassuringly promised. "Get fit. Do we have a deal?"

"We have a deal," she agreed, smiling at him while propping herself up on her elbows. One bright star in particular twinkled overhead, and for a moment, she wondered if it was the star from the Christmas story. "So, where were we before you tried to murder a defenseless little old lady? We've got Dasher and Dancer . . . Is Bashful a reindeer?"

"That's a dwarf," John replied, giving her a look. "There's Olive, though. They mention Olive in the Rudolph song."

"In what song?" Anna looked confused. "Because unless you've heard a different version of Rudolph from the rest of the world, there's no Olive the Reindeer."

"Yeah, she's the one who laughs at him," John insisted. *"Olive the other reindeer used to laugh and call him names."*

Anna threw her head back, cackling with laughter. John really was the best friend she'd ever had. He always knew just how to cheer her up. She was firmly of the opinion that everyone on Earth should have their own John.

"Olive was a dick," John said. "Bullying poor Rudolph like that."

Anna laughed affectionately, lying back down in the

snow. She smiled at him, then stared back up at that one bright star in the sky. John smiled back at his friend.

If only this moment could last forever, he thought to himself, *then everything would be okay.*

He didn't realize how right he was.

9.

THE NEXT MORNING, Anna woke up feeling surprisingly well rested. She yawned, smiling at the shaft of sunlight shining through her curtains, then rolled over to check her phone.

"*Shitwank!*" she gasped, throwing off her covers.

No wonder she felt so well rested: It was eight thirty. She'd been concentrating so hard on creeping in without waking her dad the night before, she'd forgotten to set her alarm and overslept. She had exactly ten minutes to get ready for school and get out the door, otherwise she'd be late. The last thing she needed was to spend the last day of the term in detention with Savage. Literally the least festive thing imaginable.

She showered, dressed, and while quickly blasting her hair with a hair dryer, a photograph she'd stuck to her mirror caught her eye. It was of her and her mum and dad, laughing their heads off on the log flume at a theme park they'd visited summers ago. They looked so happy. Anna felt a sudden pang of guilt. He didn't want her to go because he didn't want to lose her. All he needed was her reassurance that she'd come home, that she wasn't going to disappear from his life forever.

"Dad?" she called.

No response.

He must have left for school without her.

Anna thought of his Christmas present she'd had hidden under her bed for weeks. Months ago, she'd seen him practically salivating over some ridiculous, shiny silver toolbox in Haven Hardware but knew he'd never buy it for himself. Tony never spent a penny on himself unless he absolutely had to, and so she'd taken the money from her precious traveling fund, marched down the high street, and lugged that toolbox all the way home. She couldn't wait to see the look on his face on Christmas morning.

"Maybe John's right," she said, throwing down her hair dryer, grabbing her earbuds and plugging them into her phone as she ran out of her room. "I am getting soft."

Outside, the sun shone, and even though it was cold, the weather was bright and cheerful. Snow on the ground, a nip in the air, and only eight hours between Anna and the Christmas holidays. She stuck in her earbuds, turned up the music, and oblivious to all else, strode off down the street.

✦ ✦ ✦

John was also running late for school, but not because he'd overslept. Ever true to his word, he'd woken up early, determined to run all the way to Little Haven High School. Only ten minutes in, he'd gotten a terrible stitch in his side and now he was hobbling his way through the park, desperate to make it in time for roll call. He was leaning against the fence, about to give up and collapse on the slide when he spotted a figure that looked suspiciously like Anna Shepherd crossing the footpath toward him.

"Hey!" she called. "Check out Usain Bolt!"

John held up a feeble hand, clinging to the fence for dear life. "Get it together, son," he whispered to himself. "Get it together."

Right as he forced himself upright, the wooden slats shattered ten feet away from him and a man in a six-foot-tall snowman costume crashed through the fence, falling to the ground in front of Anna. Immediately, John righted himself and ran to her side. Anna was already on her knees, trying to help.

"Hello, can you hear me?" she asked, earbuds swinging around her neck. "I'm a first aider. I'm just going to turn you over—"

But as they rolled him, the pair jerked backward in horror. The white fleecy snowman costume was covered in sticky red and black patches and stank of something far worse than sweaty feet and cigarettes. Underneath the silk black hat, a man's face peered out of the costume, but something was very, very wrong. The whites of his eyes were red and his irises were gray, and at first, John thought he had meat smeared all around his face, but when Anna rolled him over and his jaw went slack, John realized his skin was missing. It wasn't meat, it was his bare, raw flesh. The skin from the entire lower half of his face was missing.

And then the snowman moved.

Arms outstretched, unearthly gurgling and blood oozing out of its mouth, it lurched at the pair of them. Without thinking, Anna swung her schoolbag with all her force, hitting it right in the head. With a *thunk*, the snowman tumbled back to the ground. And then it rose again.

Anna and John screamed, clinging to each other's arms and running through the playground, dodging the swings, scrambling around the seesaw, and legging it around the merry-go-round as the snowman gave chase.

Even though they'd been playing on this playground since they were little kids, they ended up trapped, stuck between the seesaw and the swings.

"Mate," John wailed, shaking from head to toe. "Come on, mate!"

"Call him 'mate' again," Anna said sarcastically, looking all around them for an escape route. "It's definitely helping."

She looked at the seesaw and then at the lumbering, blood-covered snowman. Anna had an idea.

"You stay there," she ordered John, who didn't seem entirely capable of moving, even if he'd wanted to. Anna crept slowly behind the snowman as it moved closer and closer to her friend.

"Anna?" John yelled, one eye on his friend, the other on the monstrous Mr. Frosty in front of him. "Anna? ANNA!"

Just as the snowman snatched at John, Anna pushed as hard as she could on her end of the seesaw. The other end flew into the air, the seat catching their attacker under the chin, and taking off its entire head. A fountain of blood and guts gushed up into the air as its body crumpled to the ground and the head rolled to a stop at John's feet. Still clutching his backpack to its chest, John looked down at the disembodied head in front of him.

And then he screamed. And screamed. And screamed.

✦ ✦ ✦

Two minutes later, they both sat quietly on the swings, mobile phones in their hands as they rocked back and forth in a state of shock, staring at the lifeless body of the decapitated snowman.

"No signal," Anna said, waving her phone in the air to no effect.

"Me either," John croaked as he jumped off the swing.

No one came to help when he screamed. No one sent a text to see why he wasn't at school, and he hadn't seen a single soul on his run that morning. John had a very bad feeling about this.

"Anna, that guy." He pointed to the snowman's body. And then his head, lying several feet away from said body. "He's a—"

"Don't say it," Anna interrupted.

"But he is, though."

"But he's not, though."

"He's a zombie," John finished his sentence, even though he couldn't even believe it himself.

"There's no such thing," Anna replied in denial, pushing her hair away from her face. Why couldn't she get a hold of her dad? All she wanted was to know if he was okay.

"Yeah, right. Because that's perfectly normal." He

pointed at the snowman's head. Even though Anna had most certainly removed it from his shoulders, it kept blinking and gnashing its teeth at them, still determined to put up a bodiless fight.

"It's a zombie," John said decidedly. "What else could it be?"

Anna searched for an alternative. Maybe he had rabies. Maybe it was a drug trial gone wrong. Maybe he'd had a bad mince pie and that's what really awful food poisoning looked like. Anything but the Z-word.

"This can't be happening," John said. He dropped his hands to his knees and doubled over, his breath coming far too quickly. Everything began closing in on him, and suddenly he was quite sure he was going to be sick.

There was a zombie snowman in Little Haven, and if that wasn't bad enough, it looked as though the internet was down.

"Use your inhaler," Anna instructed, rubbing her friend's back. "You're having an asthma attack."

"When was the last time you saw me with an inhaler?" John snapped. He hadn't had an asthma attack in four years, he didn't even carry an inhaler anymore. Why did she always have to see him as a child?

"Don't have a go at me just because . . ." Anna trailed off as they both looked down at the snapping head.

"Because there's *zombies*?" John finished for her.

But Anna refused to even entertain it.

"It's not zombies, don't be stupid," she said, biting her fingernails. Once again, John pointed at the head as it tried to roll itself over, using its mouth to gnaw its way along the ground to get closer to them.

"I didn't see my folks this morning," John said in a quiet, worried voice. "Did you?"

"I shouldn't have worked last night," Anna said, shaking her head. "I should have gone to the show like Dad asked me to."

John put an awkward arm around her shoulder as Anna wrapped her arms around his waist.

"Oi, are you trying to—?" Anna yelped, pushing him away.

"What? No!" John looked mortified. Mostly because he was.

A loud rumble of an explosion echoed across the town. Anna checked her phone screen again. Still nothing.

"Shit," she muttered.

"Internet might still work on my computer," John suggested. "But I don't fancy running back home, do you?"

Home was too far away, school was too far away. Anna tried to think of the closest place they could possibly get online.

"Chris's place isn't that far away?" John ventured.

"Wrong direction," Anna said, filled with cold dread for their friends. They had to get help immediately, people needed to know about this. "Do you have your keys for Thunderballs?"

John patted himself down and pulled a ring full of keys out of his coat pocket.

"All right," Anna said, leaping off the swing. "Let's go."

She paused for a moment, looking back at the snowman. Half an hour ago, she was on her way to school, and now she was looking for an internet connection to find out whether or not the world was ending. On the ground, the snowman head was munching on something. Anna and John both retched when they realized it was a dead cat.

"Suppose it might not be so bad, further into town," John said, pulling her away from the nightmarish scene.

"Yeah," Anna agreed still stunned. "Maybe you're right."

But she had a horrible feeling he wasn't.

"THAT'S ENOUGH!"

Savage blew his whistle so loudly, dogs on the other side of the Atlantic stood at attention. Everything went quiet. The assembled parents and children all shut up at once, cowering and covering their ears. Savage moved through the crowd, whistle swinging from a chain around his neck, clipboard in one hand, utterly mad power trip in the other.

According to the clock on the wall, it was five minutes to nine. Almost exactly twelve hours since he opened the doors to the parking lot after the show and saw them descending upon the school. Those monstrous, evil creatures. He barricaded the doors, he had led everyone to safety and corralled them into the cafeteria. He looked around at his dominion, aka the school lunch-room, and smiled. Dozens of parents and children all stared back at him, fear in their eyes, confusion on their faces, all of them looking to Arthur Savage to save the day. His chest swelled as he cleared his throat.

"There will be no more fighting over provisions," he barked, moving to the front of the room, every eye following him as he went. "No one eats or drinks anything without my say-so. We just need to stay calm and quiet." He paused to give Tony Shepherd a loaded look. The man could have easily doubled as a foghorn. "The government will sort all this out. There's a military base on our doorstep, it's just a matter of time until they send someone. Now if anyone has any questions, I've set up a temporary office space. By the fridge."

Keep them away from the supplies, he thought. The best way to control animals was with food. More often than not, he felt like a zookeeper instead of an educator, and never more so than today.

He turned to stare at one of the boarded-up windows, fully aware of what was out there. Most of these people hadn't seen them, but he had. Gray, decaying skin falling off their skeletons, open wounds and missing limbs, and those awful, dead eyes staring straight ahead. It was all up to him now. They were all looking to him to lead, and lead he would.

✦ ✦ ✦

In a quiet corner, Lisa sat beside Chris's grandmother. Bea winced as she pressed a hand against her chest.

"I'll get someone," Lisa said in a small, scared voice.

"The doctors can't fix it dear," Bea said with a weak smile. "I doubt there's much your teachers can do about it. I'm just worried about Christopher."

Lisa didn't want to admit it, but so was she.

"He's seen like every horror movie," she said, settling in next to Bea, trying very hard to keep the tears out of her eyes. "He'll know what to do."

The older woman nodded, but it would have been so much easier to agree if they'd been able to get him on the phone. Lisa would have given anything to go back to when she was just mad at him for not showing up in time for her song; now she had no idea where he was, who he was with. What if he'd been on his way to school to see her and been attacked by those *things*. A lump began to form in her throat and she squeezed Bea's hand.

"Your poor mum and dad must be going mad," Bea sad.

"They probably haven't even heard," Lisa replied, certain her parents were safe. "They're staying with my aunt Helen for Christmas and she lives in the middle of nowhere. It's so boring there, I didn't want to go with them."

"What I wouldn't give to be bored right now," Bea joked.

Raised voices across the cafeteria interrupted before Lisa could reply. She glanced up to see John's mom, Julie, talking to Savage.

"This is no good," Bea whispered, closing her eyes and resting against the wall. "No good at all."

"Our kids are still at home!" Julie said, almost shouting. "We need to go and get them!"

"Mrs. Wise, I have to insist that you lower your voice," Savage replied smoothly, clutching his clipboard in front of him and quite prepared to use it against this uppity little woman.

"Oh you insist, do you?" Julie answered, taking another step toward Savage. "And what are you going to do if I don't?"

"We're all worried." Tony stepped in between the two of them, placing a calming hand on Julie's shoulder. "But it's not safe for you to leave right now, Jules. We don't know how many there are. We don't even know *what* they are."

"John's out there," Julie replied, turning to Tony in complete desperation. "And your Anna. Tony, they're our *kids*."

It wasn't as if the thought hadn't occurred to him. He put his arms around Julie and gave her the most comforting hug he could muster. It was all he'd been able to think about, ever since Arthur had come running into the hall the night before, screaming like a little girl. The school was surrounded, the phones weren't working, and he had no idea where Anna was. She was a brave, clever, strong girl but those *things* . . . Every second he'd spent blocking up the windows and doors, they'd done nothing but hurl themselves against the glass, leaving themselves broken and bloody and still they came back for more. Relentless, as if they couldn't feel pain. All they wanted was to get inside and eat them. He'd never seen anything like it.

"Look, let's just give it a couple of hours, then we'll see." Tony was talking to Julie, but when he spoke, everyone listened. "Let people do their jobs. The best thing we can do right now is stay put."

"Exactly," added Savage, sliding in front of Tony to address the room. "Exactly like I said."

"They're smart kids, Jules," Tony said, clutching the desperate woman's hands in his own. "I'm sure they're safe indoors."

Julie nodded, her mouth disappearing a thin, grimly set line. Outside, the clawing and the moaning and the shrieks continued, and Tony really, really hoped he was right.

THE STREETS OF Little Haven were completely deserted.

Anna and John hadn't seen a single soul since they took on Frosty the Dead Man at the playground, their cell phones weren't working, and the evidence of chaos was everywhere. Front doors wide open, windows smashed in, tire marks streaking the streets, abandoned cars everywhere they looked, it was surreal. And yet, Anna still refused to accept the truth. *Always looking for a rational response,* John thought, following her down the street, clinging to the straps of his backpack as he concentrated on putting one foot in front of the other and ignoring the mayhem that surrounded them. She'd been exactly the same when her mom was sick, constantly rationalizing whatever the doctors said, always looking for proof that she would get better. It still made his heart hurt to think about how sad she had been.

"Maybe there was a gas leak," Anna suggested, stepping carefully over a fallen electric pole. "Or an electrical surge. I had my earbuds in when I was walking to school; there could have been an announcement and I wouldn't have heard it."

"Or it could be an alien invasion. Or what if it's the Rapture?" John ventured with just a bit too much enthusiasm. "And we're the last people left on Earth?"

"Why would we get left behind?"

"Because you nicked that bag of sweets from the supermarket when you were twelve and I didn't turn you in," he answered confidently. "You did this to yourself, Anna Shepherd."

"God help me," Anna muttered with a half smile before hitting the call button on her phone again. Still nothing. No texts from her dad, nothing from her friends. It was as though the entire world had been sucked up into thin air. But she didn't believe in zombies or aliens, and the last time she'd seen her weird old aunt, she'd been quite clear that the Rapture wasn't scheduled until the new year, so it couldn't be that. If only she'd been able to find her dad, she would have felt so much better.

"Um, Anna?"

"Um, John?"

She turned around to see her best friend backlit by a burning Mini Cooper.

"I really need a wee."

The passenger door of the car fell off and clanged to the ground.

"Let me get this straight. You're convinced it's the end of the world but you want to make a detour so you can have a wee?"

"Impending doom is very hard on the bladder," John replied, clutching his crotch discreetly. "And you're a braver man than me if zombies don't make you want to piss yourself."

"Lisa's two-year-old brother is a braver man than you," Anna commented, the stung pride on her friend's face completely passing her by. "And we still don't know it's zombies plural."

"Oh no?" John turned in a loose circle as they carried on cautiously down the suburban street. "So where is everyone?"

They turned a corner and Anna blinked at the street sign. They were on Haven Grove. "Hang on, isn't this Lisa's street? John, she might be there!" Anna began to pick up the pace down the street in hopes of finding her friend. Seeing that the thought hadn't really registered with John yet, she followed up quickly with: "And she's definitely got a landline."

"And wifi," John agreed. "And she'll definitely have a toilet."

"Honestly," Anna muttered with a grin as she ignored what looked like a pile of spoiled haggis on the lawn in front of number seventy-two. "I still don't know how men managed to run the world for so long when they can't control their bladder for more than fifteen minutes at a time."

"I don't think I've been around to Lisa's house since her mom remarried," John said, bending down to pick up an abandoned iPhone. There was no signal, but a quick swipe through the music library showed loads of Ariana Grande. John slipped it into his backpack. Couldn't hurt to hold on to it until they found its owner. And if they didn't happen to come across them, he and Anna could jam out to "Dangerous Woman" while they rebuilt the planet. If they were the only humans alive, at least he wouldn't have to be embarrassed about his taste in music anymore.

"I've only been once or twice," Anna admitted. "We always hang out at my house. Considerably fewer toddlers."

"A definite bonus," John confirmed. "Let's go to Lisa's,

we'll see if she's there, and if she isn't, try to call Tony and my mom, I'll use the loo, grab some snacks, and then . . ."

"I don't know why you can't just knock on a door and use anyone's loo," Anna pointed out. "If you were that desperate you'd just go wherever."

"Um, because it's rude?" John suggested, slapping her lightly on the back.

"I think good manners are suspended in the event of a zombie apocalypse," she replied, slapping him back and immediately stumbling over someone's abandoned suitcase.

"I thought it wasn't a zombie apocalypse," he said, grabbing hold of Anna's arm to steady her. "Thought it was a gas leak."

"It's not zombies," she repeated.

"God, look at that place," John said, nodding across the street. "Who lives there, Norman Bates?"

Anna followed his gaze and grimaced.

"For all intents and purposes, yes," she responded.

Every house on the street had *some* kind of demonstrable Christmas spirit. It was a small village without a lot of cultural variety. Pretty much everyone was Christian and celebrated the big *C*. There were one or two houses that had really gone to town with light-up sleighs hanging from the roof, giant trees drowning in baubles, even the odd pair of legs sticking out of the chimney, and sure, the decorations looked a *little* out of place in the cold post-apocalyptic light of day, but still, everyone had something, even if was just a string of lights in their window or a wreath on their door. But there was one house that stood out above all the others. The door had a rather large bolt on the front, the windows were unbroken, and there wasn't so much as a single piece of tinsel celebrating the season. Gray curtains at the windows, gray paving slabs in the front yard. John felt a chill just from looking at the place.

"But it's the most wonderful time of the year," he said, rubbing the goose bumps that prickled up on his arms. "What's wrong with them?"

"You tell me," Anna said, shivering as they walked on. "That's Savage's house."

"Ohhh," John exclaimed. "Fuckity-bye, Mr. Savage."

It made perfect sense. Any kind of decoration would require an ounce or so of imagination, and Savage saved all that for his creative punishments. He'd once made John paint the boys' locker rooms as detention because, as Savage put it: "You're such a talented artist." Wouldn't have been so bad if he'd given him a proper paintbrush instead of making him use tiny brushes from the art room. Or if the rugby team hadn't been changing at the time. He'd never been whipped with so many wet towels in his entire life.

"I know it's a terrible thing to say," he said with a huff. "But if it is zombies, I hope they get him."

"That *is* a terrible thing to say," Anna replied, linking arms with her friend. "Besides, how would you be able to tell the difference between Zombie Savage and the normal one?"

"Good point, well made," John said. "Now seriously, where's Lisa's house, because I'm two seconds away from pissing my pants."

"End of the world and he still can't go behind a tree," she teased. "It's the one with the candy-cane fence around the front garden."

"Good," he said, picking up his pace and dragging her along. "Because I don't want to have to add an additional stop to our quest."

"If you wet yourself, I'm going to make you wear my gym shorts," she replied, chasing after him as he started up Lisa's garden path.

"Lisa, are you in there?" Anna called, knocking on the front door while John did the pee dance by her side.

"I'll knock it down," he offered.

"You'll break your foot," she told him, blocking his way.

"No, it'll be fine," John insisted, working himself up for the manly display and only momentarily wondering whether or not his bladder control was up to such a feat of strength. "On the count of three."

"Three," Anna whispered, pressing down on the handle and opening the door. It was unlocked. Lisa's front door was never unlocked. Her stepdad was a policeman and her mom was always at home with the baby. They would never leave the door open.

"Totally could have kicked it down." John sulked as he pushed Anna out the way and ran into the downstairs bathroom. "Oh bugger, the door doesn't lock."

"Well, don't worry, I wasn't planning on coming in," Anna called. "Literally the last thing I ever want to see."

John said nothing.

"I can stay here and guard the door if you'd like?" she offered, screwing up her face at the sound of him peeing.

"No!" John shouted, midflow. "I mean, I don't need you to. Guard me, I mean."

"Okay, okay," she whispered to herself, taking slow and steady steps through the silent house.

The place was empty, but it didn't look as though anything terrible had happened there. It just looked as though they'd gone out and forgotten to lock the door. Anna peeked into the living room and saw the telephone resting on a side table.

"Yes!" she exclaimed, holding the receiver to her ear

and rejoicing at the sound of a dial tone. "John, what's the school's number?"

John walked through the living room door with a relieved but blank expression on his face.

"You said try a landline!" Anna said, wielding the receiver accusingly.

"I didn't say I knew the number!" John replied. "Use their wifi and look it up."

"I don't have the password." Anna opened the internet on her cell and there was nothing. "Lisa says her stepdad changes it every week so the neighbors can't steal it."

"Bollocks," John muttered, disappearing into the kitchen. "That's what you get for having a policeman in the family. Always so suspicious."

"It certainly doesn't help us right now," she agreed, closing her eyes and racking her brain for another number, any number. When she opened them, she saw John was already halfway through a banana.

"What?" John said, his mouth full. "I need my potassium. I don't want to get a cramp if we have to run."

He threw himself into a demonstrative lunge and felt something in his lower back click. He'd be regretting that in the morning.

"We should check upstairs," Anna said, reluctantly hanging up the phone. No one was answering, not even the police. Possible Rapture was looking more and more likely. John chugged a glass of milk and nodded.

"Oh sure, why not?" John muttered, following her upstairs, creaking step after creaking step. "Because nothing bad ever happens when people go upstairs to investigate in horror movies."

All the bedroom doors were open, and all the bedrooms were empty. Lisa's bed was still made, her pajamas neatly folded in a pile on the pillow. Anna reached under the mattress and pulled out her diary, turning to the latest entry. December 21.

"She didn't come home last night," she said, her shoulders sagging.

"I've got to pee again," John said, backing out of the girly bedroom. Something about being in there just didn't feel right. "Be right back."

"After we find my dad, we're taking you to see a doctor. Something's not right with you," Anna called, placing Lisa's diary carefully back where she found it. "Hurry up!"

She sat on the bed and kicked the door closed to block out his bathroom sounds, just in case he wasn't only peeing after all. Even best friends had lines that shouldn't be crossed. She looked over at the framed photos on Lisa's dresser. There were loads of her and Chris. Dressed up for a wedding, camping in the Highlands, slow dancing at the school dance. Then there were the ones of her family, Lisa and her mom, back when Lisa was a little girl. Lisa dressed as a bridesmaid at her mom's wedding, and then a more recent one, her stepdad in his police uniform, hand on her mom's shoulder, the new baby in her mom's arms, her stepbrother, Jason, sulking on one side, and Lisa standing slightly off to the other, not quite managing a smile. Anna knew things hadn't been the same for Lisa since her stepdad and stepbrother came along. Jason was older than Lisa and thought he knew everything about everything, even though Anna and Lisa had devoted considerable amounts of time to online stalking the fool and uncovered his secret pastime as a competitive roller-disco dancer. The baby was only two, but that was still fairly irritating.

But at least she had Chris. Anna stood up and smiled at the dozens of photos jammed into clip frames and hung on the wall: The two of them dressed as Disney princesses at a costume party from forever ago; Lisa, John, and Anna trying to make a human pyramid in the back garden; Anna and John singing karaoke at his last birthday party. She paused and pulled one of the pictures off the wall. A shot of her, Lisa, Chris, John, and her dad, all of them grinning in front of their Christmas tree. Anna remembered it. John's mom had snapped the photo at their annual Christmas Eve dinner a year before. Chris had his arms around Lisa's neck, John was wearing an entirely different ugly sweater, and Anna and her dad beamed at each other. Everyone looked so happy.

"How was this a year ago?" she whispered, her eyes beginning to burn at the edges. All she wanted was to speak to her dad. Slipping the photo out of the frame and into her back pocket, she caught her reflection in Lisa's mirror, all pale and blood spattered. She sniffed deliberately, and her hand hovered over Lisa's lotions and potions until it landed on a pack of cleansing wipes. Staring at herself, she wiped away any trace of what had happened and tossed the offending wipe in the bin. *There,* she thought, straightening her hair and shaking off her shoulders.

All better.

✦ ✦ ✦

Lisa's upstairs bathroom looked as though it had been decorated by Barbie. Everything was pink—pink toilet, pink sink, pink bathtub, pink shower curtain pulled all the way out so you could properly appreciate the ruffles. Even the carpet and the blinds and the towels were pink. John felt as though he were going back inside the womb.

"Ah, come on," he muttered, staring straight ahead at a rather oddly placed, framed painting of Lisa's dead grandmother. *Who hangs that kind of thing over the toilet?*

He looked down and gave his penis a stern stare. Of all the times to get stage fright. You couldn't mess about in the bathroom if you were with a girl, otherwise they'd think you were not there to pee, and the last thing he wanted to do right now was kill the romance. Because even John was well aware, the end of the world was the best chance that he would ever have with Anna. *Silver linings and all that,* he thought, pushing up onto the balls of his feet.

Reaching across to the pale-pink pedestal sink, he turned on a tap and felt himself relax at the sound of running water. Crystal streams, babbling brooks, waterfalls crashing against rocks, and *ahh,* there it was. He closed his eyes and whistled loudly, trying to drown out the sound, until a quiet rustling behind the shower curtain on the opposite side of the room made the hairs on the back of his neck stand on end.

"Lisa?" he whispered hopefully.

No answer.

"Lisa's mom?"

Nothing.

"Officer . . . Lisa's stepdad?"

A gray hand reached around the shower curtain and ripped it back, tearing it from its hooks and draping what was once Lisa's stepbrother in cascades of sugar-pink ruffles. Slowly but surely, it sat upright and turned its glazed-over eyes toward John.

"Argh!" John screamed, turning around and sending a yellow stream straight into the zombie's eye. Oh sure, *now* he couldn't stop himself.

The Zombie Jason opened its mouth and roared.

"Sorry!" John automatically yelled out of habit, staggering backward and bumping against the hard-angled edge of toilet paper holder. "Didn't mean to pee on you!"

He reached down for the waistband of his trousers, but couldn't quite manage the zip, still stumbling out of the bathroom as the zombie tried to climb out of the tub. One arm over the side, then one leg, all the while, its dead eyes fixed on its prey.

"Anna!" John screamed, struggling with his fly. "Get out! We've got to get out!"

"What's wrong?" She emerged onto the landing, clutching one of Lisa's stuffed toys, her eyes red and swollen.

Anna saw him running at her full speed, trying to pull up his trousers, and screamed too.

"For God's sake, man," she yelled. "Put it away."

"Zombie!" John yelled, desperately trying not to get bitten and also make sure his junk was safely tucked away.

It would be just his luck to get bitten by a zombie because he caught his balls in his zipper on the way downstairs. "There's a zombie! It's Disco Jason."

Quick as a flash, Anna snapped into action. She tossed the teddy bear back into Lisa's bedroom and bolted across to the bathroom door, yanking John out by his collar. Before slamming the door shut, she took a quick glance inside and felt herself turn green. It was definitely Jason, head to toe in his shiny disco gear, only now the shiny white satin shirt was covered in blood. She held on to the handle for a moment, trapping him inside as John recovered. The two exchanged a glance and sprinted down the stairs while the thing in the bathroom clawed and scratched against the wooden door like a feral cat.

"Anna," John began.

"Don't say it," she warned, pushing her hair back behind her ears and marching out the front door and down the street, every part of her on high alert.

"But it definitely was," John protested.

"I know what it was," Anna replied, refusing to cry. "And I know who it was."

"It's not him anymore," he said quietly. "Come on. We've got to get to the bowling alley."

Anna nodded, eyes trained on the horizon. An acrid scent filled the air, and a tall black funnel of smoke blew away into pale, gray clouds that filled the skies over Little Haven.

"John?" Anna said in a small, little-girl voice.

"Yeah?"

"I really want to find my dad."

"We will," he promised. "And my mom."

"Okay," she said, biting her lip and smiling at her best friend. "I'm glad you're here."

Silently, he reached out for her hand, squeezed it once, then let go as they walked on together.

"OPEN THE DOOR!" John shouted as Anna fumbled with the keys to Thunderballs. "Open the door!"

"I'm trying!" Anna replied, her hands shaking as she worked the padlock.

Behind them, a small army of blood-covered zombies staggered in their direction, slowly but surely coming closer and closer. John pressed his back against his best friend, backpack at the ready, determined to fend them off when—*click!*—Anna found the right key and the lock sprang open. They fell into the bowling alley and locked the door behind them as the mass of undead bodies roared with anger outside.

"Argh!" John shrieked as two bodies jumped up from behind the shoe counter. Anna hit the lights and sighed her first real sigh of relief. It was Chris and Steph.

"Told you it was them!" Chris said, almost falling over his own feet to get to his friends. "I saw you out the window."

But Steph wasn't so easily pleased.

"Have you been bitten?" she demanded, holding a fire extinguisher over her head. "Show me!"

"They're fine," Chris insisted, and although he didn't know it for sure, he needed to believe it was true. Anna pulled up her sleeves and turned her head to show Steph her unbitten arms.

"We're clean," she said, rolling down her sleeves. She wanted as much of her own flesh covered as humanly possible. Steph lowered her weapon but kept it close by.

"You break in?" Anna asked.

Steph shook her head. "Back door was open," she explained.

Anna gave John a look.

"That's the cleaner's job! Mrs. Hinzmann locks up the back, not me!" he replied, leaping to his own defense. "Although, she might have been concussed . . ."

"Have you heard from Lisa?" Chris asked, so much hope in his voice.

Anna and John shook their heads at the same time.

"We went to her house," Anna said slowly. "She's not there."

"But her stepbrother was," John said. "Chris, man, I don't know how to tell you, but—"

"He's been turned?" Steph guessed.

"I'm sorry," Anna said, giving Chris a hug.

"Oh no." He frowned for a moment and then broke out into his standard sunny smile. "Oh well. He was a bit of an arsehole anyway, wasn't he?"

No one could really argue with him. Jason was a complete tosser and everyone knew it.

"I'm glad you guys are okay," Steph said stiffly, setting down the fire extinguisher with great reluctance. "Whatever's going on is total insanity."

"How come you ended up here?" Anna asked, walking quickly around the room, turning on as many lights as possible.

"We were out filming the soup kitchen," Chris explained. "It was going really well, too, we had loads of good footage."

"And then somebody screamed." Steph's expression soured with the memory and Anna could only imagine. All those people in such a small space? It had to have been a bloodbath. "This was the first place we came to and Chris thought maybe you guys would still be here."

"Yeah." He looked at the floor, sadness washing over him. And then he looked up at his friends with a giant smile on his face. "But hey, zombies, right? Crazy."

John couldn't help but smile. You could always trust Chris to find a silver lining. Even if that lining was to be excited about zombies. Anna shook her head and threw her schoolbag down onto the shoe counter with a heavy sigh.

"You'll have to excuse Anna," John said. "She's in Egypt."

Steph raised an eyebrow.

"Because she's in denial."

Chris immediately held up his hand for a high five. No one loved a pun as much as Chris.

"You're not funny," Anna declared. "Have you guys heard anything? From anyone?"

"Wifi's spotty but check it out." Steph opened her laptop and they crowded around the screen, Anna with a lump in her throat. They clicked from tab to tab to tab, *The Guardian*, *The New York Times*, *Le Monde*, the BBC, CNN . . . It seemed as though Steph had checked every news outlet on the internet, and none of them had good news. GLOBAL STATE OF EMERGENCY DECLARED. ARMY DISPATCHED TO ASSIST SURVIVORS. IS THIS THE END? She settled on a site still streaming video and clicked the screen to turn up the volume.

"Governments worldwide are coordinating a response and setting up safety zones. The cause of this outbreak of violence is, as of yet, still unknown," the reporter announced.

"Yeah, sure," Steph muttered. "Big pharm has been doing weird shit for years. It's a cover-up."

"Survivors have been instructed to monitor social networks for their nearest evacuation zone and await assistance."

"Ours is the school," Steph said as the video froze.

"So the school's okay?" John asked.

"Yeah," Chris confirmed with a nod. "Lisa posted something on Facebook a while back, there's loads of people there. Her and my gran and your mom and your dad, Anna. I haven't been able to get hold of her, but they were all safe a few hours ago. The army's gonna escort us. How cool will that be?"

Anna turned to John with tears in her eyes and fell into his reassuring hug. Her dad was okay, they were going to be okay. John rested his face on the top of Anna's head and tried not to smell her hair.

"Oh *shit*!" Chris gasped.

Anna felt John's arms tense around her.

"What?" Steph gripped her fire extinguisher tightly as Chris held up his phone for them all to see.

"Justin Bieber is a zombie!" he announced with disbelief. John's jaw dropped open as he grabbed Chris's phone out of his hand to see the news for himself, while Anna and Steph shared a despairing look. This was not going to be simple.

"Also, search hashtag 'EvacSelfie,'" Chris said, peering at Instagram over John's shoulder. A stream of images appeared on the phone, hundreds of posts from people using the puppy filter as they were loaded into army vans, pulling a duckface, and throwing up peace signs next to the undead. Steph shrugged.

"We deserve to go extinct," she said simply.

As John scrolled down to a picture of a woman applying false lashes while a zombie tried to smash in her bathroom window, Anna couldn't help but agree.

"Lots of places still haven't been secured," Steph said, mentally checking off location tags. "Did you see Toronto on there?"

"Your girlfriend'll be fine," Chris promised. "And your folks. Maybe there aren't any zombies in Mexico? Bet the government is just starting with the people who need them the most."

"Sure," Steph said, closing her laptop with a snap. "Just like they always do."

13

OVER AT THE school, Justin Bieber's well-being was not the most pressing topic of conversation.

"We are not opening the doors!" Savage yelled, blocking the exit to the cafeteria with his skinny body. Tony stepped up to the increasingly manic man while everyone else watched.

"We've waited long enough, Arthur," he argued. "We're going to get our kids before it gets dark."

It had been hours. The school had lost internet service, their mobile phones weren't working, the sun was about to set, and there had been no sign of Anna or John.

"If I hadn't acted so quickly last night, those things would have gotten us." Savage shoved Tony out of the way and barked at the rest of his captives. "Now these idiots want to let them in!"

The parents in the cafeteria drew their children closer toward them as Tony and Julie stood firm behind Savage. In their quiet little corner, Lisa took Bea's hand in hers. It was cold and clammy, but the old lady gave her a brave smile.

"My girl's out there, she needs me," Tony said, as much to himself as everyone else. He turned to Savage, eyeing the ring of keys that hung from his belt. "It's not something you would understand."

Savage inhaled sharply. He stared down the other man, cold, blue eyes narrowing.

"There are creatures on the outside trying to get in," he snarled, shoving Tony again and staring down the panicking parents. "We cannot open those doors to disaster. I say we keep the doors locked and protect the people who are already safe. Face it, Shepherd, anyone on the outside is already as good as gone."

With a sharp sob, Julie collapsed to the floor. Tony knelt down to help her as Savage continued with his rally.

"We must stand our ground here; leaving the school would be suicide!"

"I will not leave my child out there to those monsters!" Tony bellowed as his voice and his temper finally broke. Several of the parents jumped at the sound of his shouting. It wasn't something they were used to hearing.

"We've got to at least try to help, haven't we? Otherwise we're no better than monsters ourselves."

A mutter ran through the crowd, mothers and fathers with their arms around their children, raising quiet objections to the idea of opening the barricades, while those without their family faintly insisted they be allowed outside.

"You can't let them in here!"

Tony looked up to see Gavin, the local butcher, comforting his son in his arms.

"They'll kill us all!"

"And what about everyone else out there?" asked another parent, Sharon. "There's not even a hundred of us in here; that means there are thousands of our friends and family and neighbors on the outside, and we've no way of knowing if they're safe. Can you honestly just sit here, twiddling your thumbs and waiting for someone to show up to save you, when you know they're all out there on their own?"

"It's the only thing we can do," Priya, a woman who lived two doors down from Anna and Tony, said quietly. Her little girl cuddled in tightly against her legs.

"I don't know how you're going to look yourself in the mirror tomorrow," Sharon replied. "I don't know how you can all live with yourselves."

"Let's see if we even make it to tomorrow," Gavin said

as he stepped forward, forcing Sharon to back down. "We're not opening the doors."

"I think it would be best if we all tried to work together," Lisa tried, but her quiet voice was drowned out by the increasing volume of the crowd.

Savage smirked as the parents turned on one another. One by one, they let go of the pretense of politeness and let their true selves show. And their true selves wanted to survive. But his satisfaction was short-lived.

"Open the door or give me the keys," Tony ordered quietly, holding his arm in a viselike grip. "Or I swear to God, Arthur, I'll throw you out to them myself."

The loud screech of a megaphone suddenly cut through the cacophony of raised voices and crying children.

"Please stay indoors," a voice ordered. "The armed forces are securing the area. Please stay indoors."

Everyone fell silent. Tony let go of Savage's arm as he backed away, sneering.

"At times like this, people need a leader," Arthur said, his voice soft and dangerous. "We can't just let people do whatever they want, Mr. Shepherd. They don't know what's best for them. In times of crisis, they need a firm hand to direct them to the right decision. So please sit down."

Tony glared at him, the anger and frustration still in his eyes. Savage took a step away from the larger man before puffing out his chest and tapping on his clipboard.

"Everyone is to remain calm," he barked. He was back in charge. "And everyone is to do as I say."

Lisa gave Tony a half smile as he sank against a table with his head in his hands.

"We'll be all right," she whispered to Bea. "They're coming for us now."

But Bea didn't answer.

✦ ✦ ✦

Before Thunderballs was a bowling alley, it had been a shoe factory. Anna had seen photos, but she still couldn't quite imagine it. Thunderballs was so loud and obnoxious with its terrible sound system and the hilarious graffiti-inspired art on the walls. It looked as though someone's dad had seen some real graffiti once and then asked a painter and decorator to do something a bit similar. The ceilings were low and there weren't many windows and even with every light in the place turned on, it still felt like perpetual twilight inside. The shoe factory had closed down before she was born, but John's mom still asked John if he was going to the factory whenever he had to work, and it always made Anna smile. John's mom was lovely. Anna paced up and down in front of the shoe counter, trying not to wonder whether or not Julie was okay.

The four of them, John, Chris, Steph, and herself, had been locked inside for hours now, and no one had come to help them. As far as she knew, no one had any idea that they were even there. The internet had gone down completely, and none of their messages would send.

She glanced out the darkened window and saw hordes of those things swaying around. Every so often one would bump into another, and they would just turn and set off in a different direction until they disappeared from sight. But there were always more. She hugged herself and sent up a silent prayer to whoever might be listening. John and Chris sat at one of the little plastic tables, munching on packets of crisps they had liberated from the stockroom. Despite the confirmed apocalypse, they were debating their theories as to which superheroes would be able to survive a zombie attack, while inhaling bag after bag of Cheetos. For some reason, Anna didn't have the stomach for snacks.

✦ ✦ ✦

Steph was struggling.

She sat and listened to Chris and John for as long as she could before she had to ditch them and now, here she was, spending what was more likely the last few hours of her life, hiding in a bathroom while two idiots argued over whether or not Deadpool's regenerative properties would save him from a zombie bite. She should have gone to Mexico. Or Toronto. Anywhere would have been better than dying in a bowling alley that looked like it was straight out of the 1980s.

She stared at the blank page in her notebook, trying to think of the right thing to say. She had to document this. She had to tell their story. So far, she'd abandoned the headlines "The End of Everything" and "What Next?"

"Too clickbaity," she muttered, crossing them out and turning the page.

She pulled off the cap of her pen with her teeth and scribbled down *A Survivor's Story*.

"Too optimistic," she sighed, capping her pen. "Too bad we don't have Deadpool to help us."

Dropping the notebook, she turned on the cold tap and let the water run before leaning over and splashing her face.

"Hey."

She jerked upright to see Anna's reflection right behind her in the mirror.

"Shit!" Steph exclaimed, her heart pounding. "What's

wrong, did you decide things weren't creepy enough already?"

"Sorry," Anna offered, turning on a tap at the neighboring sink and holding her hands under the water. Steph watched as the white of the sink turned red.

"Here." She pulled a packet of cleansing wipes out of her bag and offered them to Anna.

"Any luck getting hold of your parents?" Anna asked, nodding at the phone next to the sink.

"Mexico is not picking up," Steph replied, holding her platinum-white hair away from her face to dab at a particularly stubborn bloodstain. It was super annoying; she'd only just bleached her hair, and now it was going to need doing all over again. Someone at whichever pharmaceuticals company was responsible for this was getting a bill for a bleach-and-tone appointment come January.

"So, I was thinking this is the worst Christmas ever," Anna said, looking back at Steph in the mirror. The other girl met her eyes as she scrubbed at her face. "And then I remembered the time I got *Encyclopedia Magazine* in my stocking when I was thirteen. Aardvark to cuttlefish. My dad got me a year's subscription and to this day, I have no idea why. I'd asked him for a bike. Worst Christmas ever."

Steph mustered a chuckle.

"Just before they left for Mexico, to make themselves

feel better about leaving me here for the holidays, my folks came to visit and took me on a surprise trip," she said.

"Ooh," Anna replied. "Fancy!"

Steph turned to face her new friend.

"They took me to Birmingham."

"What?"

"One of Dad's business meetings," Steph explained, still not quite over the experience. "Mom was all, 'What's wrong? It's a city break!' Did you know Birmingham's first canal opened in 1769?"

"I did not," Anna said, tossing her used face wipe in the bin.

They both smiled until Anna caught herself in the mirror, and the happy moment fell away.

"I was horrible to my dad yesterday," she said. "Like, really horrible."

Steph stared deep into her own eyes.

"One time isn't so bad," she said quietly before looking away and hurriedly throwing her things back into her bag.

✦ ✦ ✦

"Bollocks," Chris declared. "He's a zombie."

"Robert Downey Jr. has, like, a billion dollars," John argued, still in his stained Christmas sweater. The lights flickered on and off in time to music no one could hear every time he moved. "He's in the Jacuzzi right now, surrounded by electric fences. And supermodels."

John and Chris were not in a Jacuzzi. They were in the forbidden ball pit, tossing brightly colored plastic balls at each other's faces. It wasn't exactly a "pit" but rather a blow-up swimming pool serving as a pit. John'd had dreams about this ball pit. He had longed to get into it ever since Thunderballs opened, but even back then, he was already too tall. He wasn't sure if it was the heightened emotional situation or the fact he'd wanted to get in here since he was twelve years old, but even if he was being brutally honest, it exceeded expectations.

"Just takes one personal trainer with a bite and then—" Chris held out his arms and did his best zombie impression. Which John had to admit was pretty good.

"Nuh-uh." He refused to accept it. "Iron Man lives."

"All right." Chris lobbed a red ball at his friend, choosing not to think about the sticky substance on his hand. For the first time in history, he hoped it was blood. "What about Ryan Gosling?"

"Alive, dead, the guy's still cool," John answered.

"The Rock?"

"Probably got bit trying to save people," John said, sucking the air in through his teeth. "He's just that kind of a guy."

Chris considered this for a second before accepting his answer.

"Taylor Swift?"

"Jesus, Chris!" John leaped to his feet, showering the other boy with balls. "Why would you even say that? Tay-Tay is fine!"

"Yeah, all right," Chris said, staggering to his feet. "I was just—"

"She's fine!" John shouted. "Tay-Tay is fine, Meredith and Olivia the cats are fine, and oh my God, you're a sick man, Christopher! Sick in the head!"

Chris watched as his buddy marched off, his face falling as he went.

"You don't think they're hurting cats, do you?" he asked in a little voice.

✦ ✦ ✦

In the ladies' bathroom, Anna dialed her dad's mobile number again. Steph perched on the edge of the sink, flipping the pages of her notebook back and forth while they waited for the answering service to kick in. This was the seventeenth time she'd tried; Steph was keeping count. She had a solo bet that they'd make it to twenty before Anna gave up.

"One more time," Anna said, hanging up and pressing redial. Just as the call started to ring out, there was a splash in the farthest stall. Both of them jumped and silently screamed. Anna pressed the phone against her chest as they went to investigate, together. Slowly, so slowly, Steph pushed the door open with her foot as Anna held her breath. There was someone inside. Pausing for just a second, Steph reached down and found Anna's hand. They'd been in the bowling alley for hours. Steph and Anna had been in the restroom for ages. Anyone who was still hiding in there was hiding for a reason, unless . . . unless it was—

"Mrs. Hinzmann," Anna said, breathing out heavily. "It's the cleaning lady. She must have fallen asleep."

"Oh, okay," Steph said, laughing awkwardly. "Time to wake up, Mrs. Hinzmann, it's the end of the world."

And then her eyes snapped open. Red, gray, and completely vacant. It was already too late for Mrs. Hinzmann.

"Run!" Anna screamed, but Zombie Hinzmann burst out of the stall, grabbing at the pair of them. Anna and Steph each grabbed an arm, trying to force her back into the stall, keeping as much distance as possible from her gnashing teeth. But undead Mrs. Hinzmann was a lot stronger than the senior citizen they'd left mopping the floors the night before.

"She's got some guns on her for a cleaning lady," Steph choked as Hinzmann grabbed both of them by the throat. All three of them crashed into a freshly plastered wall, leaving a giant crack right down the middle, not to mention the imprint of Anna's and Steph's skulls. Anna opened her eyes to see Mrs. Hinzmann rising slowly to her feet and zeroing in on Steph. She rolled over and knocked a dazed Steph out of the way before shoving Mrs. Hinzmann forward into the hand drier. It whirred to life, blowing Hinzmann's hair into a frizzy halo, and her loose skin rippled up in waves. As Anna tried to catch her breath, Mrs. Hinzmann charged, but this time, Steph was ready. She hooked the cleaner around the waist and hurled her back into the stall. She landed face-first in the toilet bowl.

"Gah!" Steph exploded, slamming the toilet seat down onto Mrs. Hinzmann's head over and over and over as blood sprayed up, saturating her white shirt and gray sweater with streaks of brains and gore. Anna watched as Steph continued to pound the seat onto Mrs. Hinzmann's head until there was nothing left to pound.

And then it was over.

Anna stared in horror at the carnage in the bathroom. The white walls were streaked with blood, as was Steph's face. The newly plastered wall had a crack running from top to bottom, and Mrs. Hinzmann's lifeless legs were stretched out on the floor as the stall door flipped slowly back and forth. It would take hours to clean this place up, and they'd just decapitated the cleaner. She bit her lip and considered the irony. Steph sat opposite, arms still outstretched as if she couldn't bend them, a look of sheer terror on her face.

But there was no time to recover. The bachelor party from the night before came crashing through the crack in the wall, still wearing their reindeer antlers, still obnoxiously loud, only this time, they were zombies. It was, Anna decided, marginally worse.

"Your turn," John said to Chris as his ball rolled sadly into the gutter, bypassing each and every pin. His seventh gutter ball in a row.

"I'm calling for a strike this time," Chris said, picking out his favorite ball—a shiny silver one—and lining himself up to make the shot. Just as he let go of the ball, Anna and Steph came tearing out of the restroom, screaming at the top of their lungs.

"They're inside!" Anna shouted. She stopped short, right in front of the lane as Chris's ball sailed heroically down the polished wood, charging on in a straight line. She felt every muscle in her body seize up as it collided with the pins for a strike.

"Oh God, no," Anna moaned as the UV lights lit up the entire bowling alley and the celebratory music started up at a deafening volume. She already had a Pavlovian response that made her want to punch herself in the ears every time she heard that dubstep beat kick in, and now she had to listen to this nonsense and fight zombies to the death? What a way to end a Wednesday.

The bachelor party swarmed out of the bathroom, dead eyes opening wide at the sight of fresh meat. One tried to grab at Steph, but she was too fast. This was not her first zombie rodeo. She kicked him hard and he fell backward into the front desk, fumbling at the sound system. For a moment, Anna thought even the undead were offended by the music, but no, he actually turned it up.

"They truly are evil," she whispered.

Before anyone could get even an inch closer, Anna grabbed a broom and walloped the groom-to-be in the head, knocking him clean off his feet. Slowly, she backed up toward the front door.

On the lanes, Chris was dealing with his own worst nightmare.

"Hey, it's Steve, isn't it?" he said, waving as a giant, muscle-bound zombie approached. "I recognize you from the garage, you fixed my gran's car after I accidentally filled it up with diesel."

But if Steve recognized Chris, he didn't show it. The only thing he recognized was food. The firm ground under Chris's feet gave way to the slippery polished surface of the bowling lane and he felt his feet sliding around beneath him.

"Oh no," he muttered, struggling to stay upright as Zombie Steve continued his newly unstable pursuit.

"Uh, what do I do?" John shouted as Alf, the manager of the garage, clambered over the ball dispenser toward him, festooned with tinsel and guts.

"It's like the movies," Chris shouted back, still embroiled in his own nightmare. "Destroy the brains!"

John reached into the ball dispenser and grabbed two bowling balls, one in each hand, and just as the zombie reared up at him with its mouth wide open, he swung them together, crunching Alf's skull between them.

"I did it!" John shouted over the thudding music. "I actually did it!"

Then he looked down at the mess of blood and brains and immediately vomited all over the ball dispenser.

✦ ✦ ✦

Anna swung her broom handle back and forth as the attacks kept coming. She realized decapitation wasn't enough—like with the snowman. You had to smash their heads in. *This zombie was the one who booked the party,* she recalled as she swiped at his head, *this was the best man.*

"You won't get the best of me," she promised, hitting him again. But he brushed off her swings like they were nothing. This one was stronger than the others. Back by the ball dispenser, John wiped his mouth with the cuff of his sleeve. He looked across the room and saw Anna in danger.

"Behind this!" he shouted, pointing to a table that sat between the two of them. Anna swerved around the Best

Zombie and dashed to John's side, flipping the table onto its side to create a kind of bunker. But the zombie didn't stop. He charged right into them, pushing the table and the two best friends along the floor toward the ball pit.

"We've got to jump," John commanded. "On three."

Anna nodded, her heart in her mouth.

"Three!"

Anna jumped.

"Two?"

John stared at her, still being shoved along with the table.

Only inches away from the edge of the ball pit, he dove out from behind the table. Unable to stop himself, the zombie and the table flew into the pit, disappearing under a sea of multicolored balls.

"I said after three!" John said, staring at her with disbelief.

"You said on three!" Anna corrected, rubbing her new bruises. "You need to think more carefully about your choice of words."

"'Think more carefully about your words,'" John mimicked. "I nearly got eaten by a bloody zombie!"

"And if we don't move there'll be no *nearly* about it," Anna replied, pushing herself up to her feet as the zombie rose from the balls, gurgling in anger.

John grabbed a broom of his own as Anna recovered

her weapon from the floor, and the two of them beat the Best Zombie down to his knees.

"Do it!" Anna shouted, bashing him in the head as John hovered over him with his broom handle.

"But it's gross!" John replied, waiting for the right moment until he realized there was no right moment and it was now or never, and jammed the broom handle right through the zombie's head.

Anna dropped her stick and took a step back as a pool of blood spilled out around their feet.

"Yeah, you're right," she agreed, grabbing John for a celebratory hug. "That was gross."

✦ ✦ ✦

Over at the snack counter, Steph still had problems. Brad, the zombie groom-to-be, had her backed into a corner. She felt around the counter for a weapon, a knife, a rolling pin, anything sharp or heavy, but no, all she could find was a burger spatula.

"Fuck off!" she yelped, thwipping him in the face with the kitchen utensil. But it did not put him off his mission. Running out of time, Steph took a deep breath, holding the spatula up in front of herself as he loomed above her with his jaw wrenched open, unnaturally wide, his teeth already rotten and covered in shredded flesh. Then Zombie Brad did what no one did without permission. His outstretched hands landed directly on Steph's boobs and clenched. And just when it didn't seem possible for her to hit a new level of rage, she did.

"I said, FUCK *OFF*!"

She turned the spatula around and shoved the handle up through his chin into his mouth, pushing until she felt the roof of his mouth give, and it disappeared up into his brain. She let go before he could try to bite, and the zombie slumped forward and Steph leaped over the counter to help the others.

✦ ✦ ✦

Chris was struggling. Even though he knew what to do, how to finish them off, he just couldn't bring himself to do it. But Zombie Steve was crawling along behind him, grabbing at his ankles, and Chris was out of space to run. He grabbed one of the bowling pins, taking its weight in his palm. It was heavier than he'd expected. Turning quickly, he clocked Steve in the side of the face, knocking the zombie onto his back before raising the pin high over his head, ready to do the deed. But there was something in Steve's eyes that made him pause.

"Can—can you understand me?" he asked, his arms wavering under the weight of the bowling pin.

Steve grunted and Chris could have sworn he saw him nod. There was only one way to know for sure if there was any humanity left in him. Chris would give the zombie the ultimate test.

"Who's your favorite Bond?" he asked, lowering the pin. "Most people say Connery, but for me it's—ahhh!"

Zombie Steve failed the test. He grabbed at Chris's collar and dragged himself up to his feet, opening his mouth as he smelled the sweet scent of fresh flesh at Chris's throat. Chris closed his eyes and whimpered when suddenly, he felt the zombie let go. Without wasting a single second, he ran, only stopping to look over his shoulder when he was sure he was out of reach. A perfectly played bowling ball took out Steve's legs, hitting the back of the lane and signaling a strike. The metal arm that swept the fallen pins away came down with an almighty bang, slicing off the zombie's head and sending an epic fountain of blood arcing up, high into the air. Chris looked back to the top of the lane to see Steph, still holding her bowling pose.

"Strike!" she called, busting out a celebratory dance. Until Zombie Steve's disembodied head rolled out of the ball dispenser.

"Ew." Steph frowned, stepping slowly away as the head continued to chomp and groan. "That's disgusting."

✦ ✦ ✦

For a moment, there was silence.

The foursome took in the horror all around them, the bodies scattered around the bowling alley. Steph's legs turned to jelly at the sight of the zombie massacre. She reached across the desk and turned off the music and UV lights. Somehow it looked even worse.

She slumped backward and attempted to comb some of the dried blood out of her hair, completely unaware of the zombie groom behind her, spatula still sticking out of his mouth. And then she saw him, huge and frenzied and coming straight for her. She opened her mouth to scream but there was nothing left in her. He had her cornered and she was helpless.

And then, *THUNK*.

His head snapped over to one side and he collapsed, disappearing behind the counter. Steph choked back a sob as Chris appeared, holding a bloodied bowling pin in his hand. He dropped it with a heavy thump, his easy smile completely gone from his face.

"This isn't fun anymore," he said.

Anna surveyed the scene, every inch of her body in agony. It didn't happen very often, but this time she had to agree with Chris. This definitely wasn't fun, or funny, anymore.

By the time night fell in Little Haven, things at the school had gone from bad to worse. Tony couldn't understand it, the army base was only two miles out of town. What was taking them so long? It was hours since they'd last heard anyone drive by with an announcement, and each was the same as the last: *Stay where you are, help is on its way.* But help was taking its sweet time.

The building shuddered with the sound of another explosion as the fluorescent lights of the cafeteria flickered in and out. Tony gripped the handle of his toolbox and thought about Anna. Never in his life had he felt so helpless.

"I don't know how much longer I can sit here, doing nothing," Julie said, sitting down next to him. He'd never noticed that she bit her fingernails before today; now they were practically gnawed down to nothing.

"I know, Jules," he said with what he hoped was a comforting pat on the back as another burst of gunfire echoed through the night. It was getting closer. "I wish I knew where they were."

"It's got to the point where I can't decide what would be better," Julie said with a weak smile. "Do you think there's any chance they got to the army base?"

"I think there's every chance," he said. "My Anna and your John? Unstoppable team, those two. I'll bet they got wind of what was happening last night and hightailed it out of here to get help. It wouldn't be the first time they'd done a runner, would it?"

"Remember when they ran away to join the circus?" Julie managed to laugh at the memory. "I'll never forget the look on John's face when we went to pick him up."

"Bloody clever of that clown to put them on horse shit shoveling duty." Tony nodded. "Anna cried all the way home. Ruined her new boots."

"Wherever they are, I hope they're together," Julie said, sucking the air in through her teeth. "He won't admit it but I think John's a bit sweet on Anna these days."

"He doesn't have to admit it." Tony put an arm around

Julie and she rested her head on his shoulder. "It's written all over his face. Anna's too wrapped up in this traveling nonsense to notice."

"Anna's a clever girl, she'll work it all out," she said, pulling a blanket up over their legs. "You've done a good job, Tony. Liz would be so proud of both of you."

Tony couldn't help but sniff at the sound of his wife's name.

"Aye," he replied. "I hope so. And I do hope they're together. John'll look after Anna, I know it."

"More like the other way around," Julie said, shaking her head but still smiling. "They're both going to be all right."

"They're both going to be all right," Tony repeated. "And we'll see them again soon."

✦ ✦ ✦

While everyone else huddled up in groups, sharing memories or trying to sleep, Lisa stayed by Bea's side, clutching her hand as she groaned quietly with her eyes closed.

"I'll be back in a minute." She whispered her promise into Chris's gran's ear before taking a deep breath and making her move.

"Mr. Savage?"

She stood in front of the assistant principal, who continued counting bottles of water without looking up. "I need help."

"So does everyone else, I'm sorry I have to be the one to tell you," he replied, ticking something off on his clipboard. "Typical millennial."

"Steph says we're Gen Z," she replied, immediately regretting the words when Savage looked up sharply. "I don't need help for me, it's for Bea. Is there anything we can give her?"

Savage glared at the girl but she did not waver.

"Am I supposed to know who that is?" he replied.

"She's Chris's grandmother," Lisa explained. "It's just she's got a bad heart and she hasn't got her pills and I know you've got the first aid kit and I thought—"

"Miss Snow." Savage held up a hand to cut her off. "Look around. What do you see?"

Lisa looked left, then right, then right again.

"Uh, tables?" she suggested brightly.

"You see civilization on the brink," he said, carefully enunciating each word. "But we still have the system, we have rules. And what does the system say we should do to survive?"

"Eat an apple a day," Lisa replied confidently.

Savage shook his head. The girl was an idiot.

"Help one another?" she guessed.

He leaned in until she could feel his bristly beard against her ear.

"Prioritize," he hissed before going back to counting the bottles of water in front of him.

"So you're not going to help, then?" Lisa asked, her voice shaking.

"I am helping, Miss Snow," Savage replied. "I'm helping the people who stand a chance. Now if you don't mind, I'm rather busy."

✦ ✦ ✦

Savage looked up from his position at the front of the room where he was guarding the supplies. This wasn't exactly what he'd planned to do with his Christmas break, but he had to admit, a crisis certainly brought out the best in him. He'd always suspected he was a born leader, and now it was confirmed. When this was all over, perhaps a run for local government was in order. Head of a local school was a waste of his talents. He owed it to himself, nay, the world, to take control. Besides, the way things were going, most of the kids were going to be zombies soon enough.

"The ones that aren't already," he said to himself, sniggering at his own joke.

Without warning, bright, white light filled the room, followed by an earsplitting explosion. It disappeared as quickly as it came, but the survivors in Little Haven High School began to panic.

"Stay calm, everybody," Savage called as the whispers began to rise to a rumble. "Stick to your designated areas and let the army do their job."

There was silence for a moment and then a rally of gunfire, followed by a blood-curdling scream.

"People are dying out there!" Julie yelled, clambering to her feet. Tony scrambled up right beside her, forcing a brave face. He squeezed Lisa's hand as she wiped away another stray tear. Hope was fading fast.

"It's going to be okay," he promised. "You watch Bea, I'll check the doors."

While Savage continued to bark orders, Tony grabbed his toolbox and took himself off to test the barricades.

"You keep on talking," he said under his breath. "It's all you're bloody good for."

He could see things were taking a turn for the worse. People were starting to lose faith that anyone was coming. How could it be taking them this long? The army had guns, they had tanks, they had so many weapons. There was no way they wouldn't win this.

"Just got to stay here," he said, tugging on his DIY defenses, one after the other. The barricades held firm and so did he. "People are relying on you, you big daft idiot."

But what about Anna . . . ?

It was too much. He'd been holding it together for a whole day, and he had no idea where his little girl was, no idea if she was a zombie, no idea if he'd ever even see her again. He broke down, big juddering sobs taking over his whole body as he leaned forward against the wall and let the tears come.

"Mr. Shepherd, can I get a—"

He sniffed and straightened immediately, wiping his face on his sleeve. Lisa stood behind him, mouth hanging open and feeling extremely awkward.

"Can I get a pillow for Bea?" she asked quietly.

Better not ask if he's okay, she decided. She knew he wasn't, and it seemed cruel to make him pretend.

"I'll be there in a minute, love," Tony said, keeping his back to Lisa. "Almost done here."

He checked the rest of the doors and windows; his cobbled-together defenses were as sturdy as they could be. Just as he was about to go back into the cafeteria, he saw a flash of gunfire in the near distance, someone running fast. *Could it be Anna?* Pressing himself up against the window, Tony squinted, closing one eye to get a better view between the boards he'd put up against the glass. Instantly, he wished he hadn't. The world outside that window was not one he knew. Fires raged, cars were overturned, and there were tanks just beyond the school parking lot. Tanks! But even more disturbing than the heavy artillery were those creatures. He'd seen a few of them the night before, but there were more, so many more.

He pressed closer, trying to get a better look when one of them crashed against the window, nothing but a thin pane of safety glass and his own wooden barricades holding them apart. It thrashed wildly, snapping its jaws as though it might be able to chew through the window. Its skin was gray and thin, and one of its eyeballs was missing. Tony wasn't much for scary movies, but he'd seen a couple in his time.

"It can't be," he breathed as the creature continued to bash its own head against the window over and over, patches of flesh and skin peeling away from its skull. "There's no such thing as zombies."

Regardless, he scooted away from the window and staggered back into the cafeteria.

"Tony?" Julie said as he sat back down on the floor, shaking. "What's wrong?"

"Nothing," he replied, bundling up his jacket and passing it to Lisa. "Here, it's for Bea. It's the best I can do, I'm afraid."

Lisa took the makeshift pillow with a grateful smile and slid it under the old lady's head as she whimpered quietly in her sleep. Turning his back on the room, Tony lay down and pressed the home button on his dying phone as the fluorescent lights flickered out again. A photo of Anna, looking back over her shoulder and smiling, lit up in the darkness.

✦ ✦ ✦

Thunderballs was closer to the action than the school. Still surrounded by the bodies of the bachelor party from hell, John, Anna, Chris, and Steph gathered together around the snack counter. Somehow, John found the strength to chew on a stick of beef jerky while the others watched Steph refresh her internet browser over and over. Anna stared at John with a look of disbelief. "How can you possibly be hungry?" John shrugged and finished his jerky.

The same blindingly white explosion that had rocked the school blinded the bowling alley for a split second before fading away, taking the electric lights with it.

"That's fine, right?" John said, through a mouthful of meat. His eyes adjusted to the dark far too quickly for his liking. He could still see the zombie that he'd impaled on a broomstick a couple of feet away.

"I mean, they probably need to blow things up."

"Shut up," Steph ordered, holding her breath as gunfire shattered the silence, followed by ear-piercing screams and more gunfire.

"I don't think it's fine," Anna said, checking her phone. It was just a reflex now; she didn't really expect to see any signal but she couldn't stop herself from doing it.

"Guys, look!" Steph jumped up and waved them all over to her laptop. "I got a signal!"

The news pages on the computer screen flickered to life, refreshing slowly, each line of the stories stuttering into being. As the page filled with bad news, Steph's face turned white. THOUSANDS DEAD IN MEXICO CITY. NORTH AMERICAN EPIDEMIC SPREADS. MARTIAL LAW DECLARED.

"Steph." Anna put her hand on the other girl's shoulder as the wifi signal disappeared again, filling her computer screen with a static image of chaos and despair. "It doesn't mean—"

"Yeah, it does."

She slammed the laptop shut as she cut Anna off. Brushing her hair out of her face, she pulled the sleeves of her sweater over her fingers and walked a few steps away. Anna turned to John, who was busy tucking his sweater into his trousers. Without electricity, there was no heating and without heating, it was as cold as a meat locker inside the bowling alley.

"Give her a minute," John whispered, nudging his friend in the arm as they stood side by side, staring out the tinted windows. Thankfully, it was difficult to make out exactly what was happening. Flashes of gunfire and occasional explosions lit up the scene, but even if they couldn't hear, they could see. And it did not sound like anyone was going door-to-door singing Christmas carols out there.

"I'm glad you're here," Anna said, dropping her head on her friend's shoulder. "Poor Steph."

"Yeah," John said, hardly daring to breathe. "I can't imagine not knowing if my girlfriend was still alive. If I had a girlfriend. Which I don't."

"Isn't it mental?" Anna asked, completely missing his awkward rambling. "Yesterday, I was so stressed out about going traveling. Now I don't even know if there's anywhere to travel to."

"And I'm not nearly as worried about whether or not I got into art school." John laughed. "So I suppose there's even a silver lining to a zombie apocalypse!"

"I mean, there had to be at least one," Anna said, cracking a smile before another sobering, blindingly white blast shook the building. She covered her eyes with one hand and grabbed John with the other. She had never in her life been so thankful for her best friend. Looking over her shoulder, she saw Steph with her arms around Chris, a tight smile on her face.

"You know what they say," John said with a sigh.

"You've got to hold on to what you've got. It doesn't make a difference if we make it or not."

"Yeah," Anna agreed before turning to look at her friend. "Hang on, aren't they the lyrics from 'Livin' on a Prayer'?"

"Clever old fella, that Jon Bon Jovi." John nodded.

"And I thought you'd already hit peak sad," she said, taking his hand in hers again. "Impressive, my friend."

She wasn't alone and she wasn't defeated. Just like John Wise *and* Jon Bon Jovi said, they had each other and that was a lot. Maybe there had to be a way out of this, and if there was, Anna would be the one to find it.

"OH SHIT."

Anna jerked awake and saw balls flying everywhere. It took her a moment to remember where she was and as soon as she did, she wished she could forget again. She'd passed out in the ball pit, intentionally burying herself should more zombies somehow get into the bowling alley. Luckily, that hadn't happened "What's wrong?" she asked, rolling herself forward on all fours until she reached solid ground. Chris was glued to the tinted window at the front of the bowling alley.

"The snow's gone!" he replied, genuine surprise in his voice. "I was hoping for a white Christmas."

"Fucking hell, Chris!" Anna said as Steph and John yawned themselves awake in their respective spots. "What about the army?"

"See for yourself."

He turned away from the window as Anna cupped her hands around her eyes to better see what was happening. John and Steph lined up beside her.

The army had lost. The number of zombies aimlessly wandering around in the parking lot had doubled, dozens of them wearing military fatigues. A tank stood in the middle of the street, its cannon pointing up into the sky with half of a human being hanging out of the top hatch.

"Everyone's dead," Steph said slowly.

"People will be waiting at the school," Anna said with determination. "We just need to get there."

"Look!" Steph jabbed her finger against the glass at the bloody scenes outside. "There's no evacuation coming, Anna! Everyone is dead. Everyone!"

Anna couldn't afford to start thinking that way. She just couldn't. "So we'll get your car and leave town," she answered, kneeling down to tighten her shoelace.

"And go where?" Steph asked, still staring out at the bodies scattered around on the cold concrete. Tears slowly trickled down Chris's cheeks as he turned his attention from the weather to the carnage in front of him.

"I don't know yet but we'll figure something out," Anna replied. "I'll come up with a plan."

"Oh, of course, I forgot," Steph said with her usual sarcasm. "You can do anything."

It was all too much. The bodies, the zombies, the eerie quiet, Chris's silent tears.

"I'm getting my dad, all right?" she shouted.

No one said anything.

"And my gran." Chris sniffed. "And Lisa."

Steph shook her head as she walked away. Maybe they were all the same age, but they were acting like clueless kids. The writing was on the wall, right next to the sergeant major's small intestine.

"I wanna get my mum, too," John said. The lights on his Christmas pullover had almost stopped lighting up completely. "But how do we get past all the zombies?"

"We can't stay here," Steph admitted. "We're basically an all-you-can-eat zombie buffet."

"Like at Pizza Hut," Chris replied, his eyes glazing over at the thought of unlimited breadsticks. He flicked his hoodie up over his head and watched a few loose plastic balls fly out and graze Steph in the chest.

"I could go for a meat feast right now," John rambled. "And a giant full-calorie Coke and a tub of Ben & Jerry's and a desert island with swimming pool because I hate sand and preferably no zombies."

"I've had an idea," Chris said, a grin reappearing on his face. "And it's the best idea ever."

✦ ✦ ✦

"This is the stupidest idea ever," Steph muttered, minutes later. "I want to go on record as having said that before we get eaten."

The streets of Little Haven were a living nightmare. Everything they knew and took for granted, turned inside out and set on fire. Everywhere they turned, there was a new nightmare. Soldiers ripped in two, their insides on the outside, random body parts scattered far and wide. In the distance, they saw the town Christmas tree burning like a warning beacon, telling anyone who might see it to stay away. And in the middle of it all, a bright blue overturned swimming pool / makeshift ball pit waddled down the center of the street on four pairs of very unsteady legs.

"We're all going to die," Steph said as they bumped into a wall for the umpteenth time.

Chris, at the head of the ball pit, held his phone out in front of them, scouting a clear route. It had charged a little overnight, but there was still no signal.

"Want to play a game?" John asked. "It always helps me keep my mind off of things when I'm car sick."

"Because this is exactly the same," Anna muttered, crouching low underneath the blue plastic.

"I've got it," Chris replied. "Steph, you first. Marry, shag, kill. Zombie Miley, Zombie Rihanna, Zombie Beyoncé."

"Kill all of them," Steph answered without hesitation. "They're zombies."

"Play it properly," Chris whined, guiding the gang around a stray arm.

Not for the first time, Steph looked at him like he was a complete idiot.

"Jesus, fine." She blew out a heavy breath. "Marry Beyoncé . . ."

"Why are you killing Rihanna?" John asked in a high-pitched squeal.

"I didn't say that," Steph answered, even though she was absolutely about to say that.

"Well, you're obviously shagging Mi—" John cut off mid-sentence as the ball pit thumped into something. The gang dropped to the ground, hiding their legs under the plastic pit.

"Is it a horde?" John whispered, all thoughts of his beloved pop princesses forgotten.

"How many would it have to be to count as a horde?" Chris asked, sliding his phone carefully out from under the plastic.

"Just check!" Anna hissed, tucking her hair behind her ears, scared to death but ready to fight.

He peeked at his screen. A goofy grin spread across his face. "You won't believe it."

156

"I swear, if he says the snow is gone again, so help me God," Steph mumbled.

"Uh, better!" Chris replied, turning to his friends and showing them the photo he had just taken. "Killer old people!"

They had made it to the Little Haven Restful Days Care Home, where the town's senior citizens came to rest. Or be turned into the merciless undead with an insatiable hunger for living flesh.

One or the other.

The old-aged pensioner zombies surrounded them, hobbling along with canes and walkers. One legless creature pulled itself along the ground as its entrails dragged along behind, leaving streaks of red along the concrete. It sniffed at the air and turned, slowly, toward the ball pit.

"What. The. Hell."

Steph gasped and then froze as a heavy lump pressed against her head through the wall of the ball pit. Chris angled his phone out the bottom of the ball pit and snapped a pic.

"Yeah," he whispered, taking a look at the photo. "You have an old woman sitting on your face."

He held up the phone so everyone could see. It was a particularly unflattering angle, even for a zombie. Anna peeked out from underneath her side, looking for an escape, but instead she saw the legless creature, crawling toward them, picking up pace. It snapped its teeth, the scent of fresh meat driving it along the cold ground. Anna whipped the ball pit back down onto the ground.

Steph was equally keen to get away. *Drip. Drip. Drip.* Not rain. Not now. A dribbling sound ran down the side of their cover and liquid ran right past her face.

"Wait? Is she pissing?" Steph hissed in horror.

A zombie grandma was urinating on her face.

"You're fine," Anna whispered back, far more concerned with the legless threat outside and trying to stifle a giggle at the same time. "It's plastic."

"It's *warm* plastic," Steph snapped back. "This is the worst. Wet, warm, undead old person piss. *It cannot get worse than this.*"

"Pretty cool," Chris said, tucking his phone away as they held the plastic cover down to the ground as tightly as possible. "Who knew zombies still needed to go for a wee?"

The legless zombie reached the ball pit and snarled loudly, alerting the others to the treats inside. They were under attack. Gnarled hands with skinned knuckles and missing fingernails scratched at the blue plastic, trying to get inside, trying to turn it over, desperate to feed. Anna and John pressed themselves against the ground, clinging to the edge of the ball pit, their fingers cramping with the pressure of holding on. Suddenly the hot, wet lump on top of Steph's head lifted, all at once. She straightened her neck for just a second, eyes wide with fear, before the old woman's body crashed down onto the top of the ball pit, blood oozing in every direction.

Everyone screamed.

Blood ran down the sides of the pit, turning the bright blue a dark, miserable red.

"It got worse," Steph whispered. "I apologize. Blood is worse than piss."

A loud *thunk* outside sent another body crashing into the ball pit as the gang collapsed into a pile, facedown against the floor, waiting for the inevitable.

They're turning on each other, Anna thought to herself, covering her head with her hands. *They're fighting over who gets to eat us.*

Another thud. And then another. Angry roars filled the air and then . . . laughter?

"Guys?" John turned his head to meet Anna's terrified gaze. "I think there's someone out there."

With a gulp, Anna gingerly lifted the plastic by an inch.

"Argh!" she screamed, face-to-face with the legless zombie. It opened its mouth and Anna could see the rotting flesh stuck between its teeth. She jerked back, nowhere to go, nowhere to run, but the zombie did not move. It stayed exactly where it was, snapping its jaws at her. A foot planted itself in its back, holding it in place.

"What the . . . ?" Anna muttered as someone flipped over the ball pit, leaving them exposed. A baseball bat crashed down into the legless zombie's head, smashing its skull into bloody smithereens.

"Well, that was disgusting," Steph muttered, wiping brains out of her hair.

Standing tall, his foot still planted in the back of the double-dead pensioner, was Nick. He smirked, flipping the baseball bat onto his shoulder.

"All right, losers?"

"IF YOU WERE planning to go outside, you really should have taken some muscle," Nick said, hoisting Anna up to her feet. "Oh, hi, John."

Of all the people not to have been eaten by zombies. John glowered as he climbed up to his feet.

"You're still here," Steph said, dusting herself off. Nick didn't even offer to help her up. "I thought your big army dad woulda pulled in a favor and shipped you out."

"Don't talk about my fucking dad!" Nick yelled, pointing his baseball bat at her. Steph raised her eyebrows. That escalated quickly.

"Show some respect," Nick said, pushing his dark brown curls away from his face. Somehow, the blood splattered across his face made his eyes even bluer than usual, John noted. Why couldn't he have had the decency to just die?

"Says the guy who just murdered a bunch of grandparents," Steph replied before leaning over to whisper to Chris. "We should be filming. Get that on camera, bit of human interest."

Chris nodded, turned on his phone, and began filming the massacre, his tongue sticking out the corner of his mouth. Anna was exhausted, anxious, and emotionally conflicted. She was happy to find another survivor but not entirely ecstatic to find out it was her ex-hookup. She surveyed the quiet misery that surrounded them, wondering who else could still be out there.

The silence didn't last long. Nick's horrendous friends crashed into the parking lot, hooting and yelling, each of them pushing shopping carts that were packed full to the brim.

John clocked the contents. Food, yes, that was sensible. Toilet paper, couldn't argue with that. And in the next cart, dozens of game consoles and video games.

"Oh, you've been looting," he said with measured surprise. "How lovely."

But Nick didn't react. Something was wrong.

"Nick," Anna said, lowering her voice. "Where's your dad?"

"He went off to the base," he replied, clearing his throat. "Trying to save all your arses."

She followed his gaze over to a pile of dead soldiers nearby.

"I'm sorry," she said, wondering if he knew any of them. No one looked familiar to her, but Nick had grown up on that base.

"Whatever," he replied. "I'm fine."

He wasn't fine.

Before she could press him any further, Anna heard the familiar rumble of groaning from across the parking lot. They'd waited too long. One by one, a huge group of zombies had come shambling down the ramp. Anna turned to look for another way out, but they were trapped.

"Is that enough to count as a horde?" Chris asked, still filming.

"Shit!" John grabbed the edge of the ball pit. "Everyone, get back under."

"Hiding is for pussies, John Boy," Nick replied, spinning the baseball bat in his hand. He turned to face the oncoming threat, a smile stretching across his face. "We're hunters."

He nodded over at his friends, Jake, Tibbsy, and Graham, each one bigger and stupider than the last. They reached into their carts, ripping open packaging and tearing into boxes, looking for a weapon.

"Is it me," Steph said, sidling up to Anna, "or are they excited about fighting zombies?"

Anna nodded as Graham pulled out a toilet seat and grinned.

"They're idiots," she reasoned. "So yeah, they probably are."

Anna, Steph, John, and Chris pressed together, back-to-back-to-back-to-back, looking for a way to escape. Chris stepped forward and held up his phone, ready to film, but Steph pulled him away, shaking her head.

"We gotta stay safe, buddy," she said, keeping him locked in to the group.

Alone, Nick strode out ahead, one hand holding his bloody bat, the other balled up into a fist.

"Time for a hero," he said, steeling himself for the onslaught.

Jake, Tibbsy, and Graham fell in behind him. Jake twirled a control from an Xbox like a lasso, Tibbsy clutched a handful of kitchen knives as though they were Wolverine's claws, while Graham had his arms full of watermelons.

"He carried a watermelon," Steph commented as the zombies came closer.

"He's a bloody idiot," Anna whispered as the group backed away.

"It's not that difficult if you've got the balls to fight," Nick shouted back, taking a fighting stance. "You've just got to follow the rules. Rule one, stay focused."

He pulled back his bat and prepared to strike. Rubbing her eyes in disbelief, Anna realized who he was about to attack. It was the local girls' soccer team.

"As if little girls aren't scary enough already," Chris muttered. "The under-fourteens' Undead Eleven."

"Rule number two," Nick shouted over the unnatural screeching. "Use your imagination. Have some fun."

"Jesus Christ, do we have to listen to this?" John asked. "I'd rather let them eat my brains."

Nick made eye contact with the closest zombie and grinned. Without a second thought, he pulled back his bat and smashed it straight through the girl's skull.

"If it wasn't for me, you'd already be dead," Nick called back, pointing his baseball bat at John. "While you were busy hiding, I've been kicking zombie ass for twenty-four hours straight."

Unimpressed, John gave Nick the finger.

Tibbsy and Jake were just as busy. Jake smashed up anyone who came within a three-foot radius, while Tibbsy clobbered the goalkeeper with his games controller. Graham stood still, clutching his giant fruit, seemingly with no idea of what was going on.

"I'm a soldier now," Nick shouted. Whether he was trying to impress someone or convince himself, Anna wasn't sure. "This is war; I'm a soldier at war."

"No," Anna muttered, a bit conflicted between his willingness to protect her and his demeaning, chauvinistic attitude. "Your dad's a soldier. You're a posturing, full-of-it dickhead. There's a difference."

For a brief second, all the zombies were down. Nick and his gang climbed on top of a burned-out car and shared a celebratory high five, cheering their success. But Anna knew better than to assume it was over.

"Come on," she said, nodding at Steph and Chris, then tugging on John's hand. The four of them ran for it at full speed.

Watching them go, Nick hopped off the car, jogging after Anna.

"It's all a big game," he shouted as the fleeing foursome stopped in their tracks. More zombies incoming. "I'm here to get the high score."

He pulled back his swinging arm, then froze.

It was soldiers. Undead soldiers, still in their fatigues, blood running down their faces.

"Only the toughest are going to survive this," Nick yelled, signaling for his friends to charge their carts at the soldiers. "Running away isn't going to help. The best form of defense is attack."

The shopping carts crashed into the first wave of zombies, knocking them off their feet. Tibbsy and Jake filled their arms with cans of food and pelted them as hard as they could, knocking the remaining soldiers to the ground, crushing their skulls as they went down. John fought the urge to vomit as bloody gray matter spilled all over the ground around their feet.

"We've got to get out of here," he said to Anna as Tibbsy traded his cans for a machete. "I can't watch this."

"I think they're winning," Anna replied, looking back over her shoulder as John dragged her away.

"Oh, I know." John grimaced as they ran. "That's what's so upsetting about it."

"Where are you running to, Johnny Boy?" Nick asked, manhandling a zombie into a headlock. "Stay and fight like a man!"

"Fuck. Off," John muttered, realizing Nick was at least half right. There was nowhere to run. Even if they killed all these zombies, they were everywhere.

Nick tore off his captive's head before turning his baseball bat on a whole row of monsters that Tibbsy had lured over with a piece of steak on a string, and with a warrior's cry, Graham smashed the last soldier zombie's head clean off his shoulders with his watermelon.

"That was kind of impressive," Chris admitted. Steph and Anna gave a half-hearted shrug and immediately turned to leave, strolling past a gore-stained Nick without a word.

"Come on, boys," Nick said, flicking a piece of lung off his shoulder. "Can't let these ladies go off without some real men."

"If you see any who are actually capable of getting it up," Anna called back over her shoulder. "Do let me know."

John sniggered and turned to give Nick the finger one more time. Even if they died before the day was out, he'd always have that moment.

"Ignore her," Graham said, clapping his friend on the back as the gang disappeared around the corner. "Guess only the bitches survive, right, Nick?"

Nick shrugged him off with an irritated glance.

"Shut the fuck up, Graham," he replied before breaking out into a run and chasing after Anna and her friends.

18

Morning arrived at the school with a similar sense of chaos and panic. Everyone was packed up and ready to leave, even the parents and families who had been desperate to stay. Everyone could see there was no point in staying put anymore. They were sitting ducks. As soon as the creatures outside found a way inside, they were done for.

Well, everyone except for one very loud, very insistent assistant principal.

"We must hold out until help arrives!" he yelled from his position on top of a table. He waved his clipboard in an effort to calm the shouting, but nothing helped. "I've made a twelve-point plan and if you would all shut up, I will explain it to you."

But the people of Little Haven had made up their

minds. The army had been defeated, and no one had come to their rescue. They were ready to take their chances on the outside.

"The army's gone, Arthur." Tony moved to the front of the crowd, the leader of the evacuation. "We're on our own now, it's time to go."

"We have emergency guidelines for a reason," Savage argued, his voice teetering close to hysterics. "Just look at my plan and you'll realize I'm right."

Julie slapped the clipboard out of his hands, and Savage gasped as it skidded away across the room, pages of paper flying into the air like doves. The room went silent, all eyes on Savage.

"If you love this place so much, you're welcome to stay," she said, standing shoulder to shoulder with Tony. "You'll be staying here alone."

Everyone looked away, ashamed to have listened to him for so long. Slowly they all turned to give Tony their undivided attention.

"Right, here's the plan," Tony started, clapping his hands together.

Savage felt his face turning red as anger bubbled up in his blood. What was wrong with them? How could they ignore him in favor of this imbecile? This uneducated, oafish *handyman*? He didn't even have a real job, just an ornery daughter and a body-odor problem he flatly refused to address.

"Just listen to me," he pleaded. But the words stuck in his throat. They were already gone, already turned to Tony. It made no sense, they were literally offering themselves up as sacrifices to stupidity. And all because they didn't know a superior mind when they saw it. Or worse, they did know and they didn't care.

"This is my school," Savage said in a small, soft voice to no one.

They were already gone, mentally out the doors that he had fought so hard to keep them inside of. They would never listen to him again, he realized, watching as Tony talked them through his absurd plan, his suicide mission. They'd never respect him. They never had respected him. The children treated him like a joke, the other teachers left him out, the townspeople ignored him. He had no friends, no family, no lover, not even a pet who would miss him.

He might as well already be dead.

"Arthur," Tony said, reaching a hand up to the other man. "Come with us. You can help organize—"

"Don't you condescend to me, you pathetic little man," he snapped, hissing through his teeth into Tony's shocked face. "Everything I've done for them? And what do I get?"

He strode away into a corner, arms crossed tightly

171

across his chest, eyes fixed on Tony Shepherd as he rocked back and forth.

Walking slowly away, Tony turned his attention to Lisa and Bea, while Julie went from group to group, making sure everyone had their things.

"Are we really going outside?" Lisa asked, physically shaking at the thought.

"We have to," Tony said, gently pressing Bea's hand with his own. Her hands were cold and her face was ashen. Tony didn't know what to say.

Lisa looked out at the boarded-up windows, her bottom lip trembling.

"No one's coming for us, are they?"

"Prepare yourself, love," Tony said. "We might see some very bad things out there."

✦ ✦ ✦

The fastest route to the school was through the local shopping center. It wasn't anything fancy, just a newsstand, a chip shop, the discount store, and the requisite shitty chain coffee shop. Anna almost never came down here unless her dad had a fish and chips craving. Probably no chance of a bag of fish bits now.

Graham kicked a stray mannequin lying in the street before bending over and dry humping it, much to the delight of his friends.

"Best lay of his life," Steph commented, still not altogether delighted by the new additions to their group. Nick's friends were loud and obnoxious. Loud and obnoxious attracted attention, and attention meant zombies.

They'd already been here. The storefronts were smashed in, and evidence of carnage lay all over the place. An arm here, a scalp there. A bloody handbag hanging from the bough of a tree. But so far, no more survivors.

Nick casually raised his baseball bat and smashed a shop sign, laughing hysterically as it cracked and then shattered. The thrill of violence without consequences. There was no wonder someone like him was thriving in this situation. Anna kept her distance. How could she ever have been attracted to him? That one night, that one stupid night. She always said she didn't believe in regrets, but he was really testing her commitment to that life lesson.

Not far behind, Steph and Chris filmed the wasteland, making notes, capturing content.

"Do you think they'll use our stuff on the news?" Chris asked. "My gran would be so proud."

Steph smiled weakly. She didn't have the heart to tell him that the newsreaders and his gran were probably already gone. Even though she carried on, following Anna on her quest to find her dad, Steph had already given up. Her parents were dead, her girlfriend was dead, and their chances of survival were not increased by four idiots smashing up everything in sight. They'd be dead before sunrise, she was sure of it.

At the head of the group, John pushed an empty shopping cart through the plaza. Without a word, Anna caught up to him, jumped in, and folded her knees under her chin so she was facing John. He pushed her along in silence for a moment as they took in the scenes around them.

"S'weird, isn't it?" John said, after a while.

"That's one word for it," Anna agreed.

"I mean, you hear about riots and revolutions and stuff in other countries, but not here, not on our high street. We could die."

"Hey!" She was not having that attitude.

"We could, though!" John said. "Zombies, Anna. They're real, actual zombies."

Anna let out a heavy sigh. Did he think she didn't know that?

"But at least you're not leaving anymore," John said in a cheery tone. "So at least that's something."

She reached out and put a hand on his. He immediately stopped pushing the cart, wondering if she knew how fast his heart was beating.

"What does that mean?" Anna asked.

"It's different now, isn't it?" he replied, not loving the

look on her face. "You can't go traveling now. You can't leave me."

And there it was. The unspoken thing, said out loud.

Anna leaned back in the cart and stared face-to-face with her oldest pal.

"John," she said, keeping a very deliberate distance. "You're my best friend, yeah? You know that."

"'Course," John replied. Even the tips of his ears blushed. They were best friends, they'd always been best friends. But they could be so much more, now it had all changed, he wanted to say, the words on the tip of his tongue. They could be so much more to each other.

"John."

He opened his mouth to speak as their eyes met. This was it, this was his moment.

"You're my best *friend*," Anna said. "And nothing could ever change that."

All the air went out of him at once. His shoulders sagged and something in his eyes went away. Anna bit her lip. She hated to do it, hated to hurt his feelings, but she knew that she could never feel that way about him, no matter how hard she tried. Why couldn't he see that a best friend was so much more important than a boyfriend? They would be in each other's lives forever, and she wouldn't do anything to risk that.

"Swap," John said, awkwardly stacking himself into

the cart in Anna's place. Obediently, Anna pushed him onward.

"Besides, nobody's dying," she said with confidence. "I'm going traveling and you're going to art school. You're going to be a world-famous artist and come back and buy this entire town and bulldoze the school to make room for your incredible new studio."

"Because people are really going to be in need of cartoons after this," John replied, a sarcastic and slightly sour note in his voice. She didn't want him. She'd never want him. Not even if he was the last man on Earth.

"More than ever," Anna agreed, missing his sadness, on purpose or otherwise.

"You seriously think you can still get away after all this?" he asked as they passed a travel agent office. The windows were full of pictures of palm trees and sunny beaches and snowy mountains dotted with deliriously happy people zooming down them on skis.

"Watch me," Anna replied.

✦ ✦ ✦

"I always knew I'd be good in a crisis," Nick said as they crept through the outdoor mall. "I've got all the right survival skills."

I suppose there had to be an upside to being a selfish, aggressive wanker, Anna thought to herself, but decided now was not the right time to criticize. "I can't say I've ever thought about it before."

"I always figured I'd be good in a zombie apocalypse," Steph said. "You've got to be tough, you've got to be ruthless. I just want you all to know, I'd take any one of you out if you got bit. I wouldn't even hesitate. So don't worry about it." Her protective exterior was back, although it was quite obvious this time that she was trying to lighten the mood.

"Yeah, thanks, Steph, I feel loads better now," John said, moving farther away from the platinum-haired girl as she gave a gracious but threatening nod.

"I'm good at stuff," Chris offered. "Like building fires and cooking and things like that."

"Practical skill, that's what we need in times like these," Nick said, clapping him hard on the back before turning his attention to John. "What about you, John Boy? You going to draw a nice picture of the end of the world?"

"I can do loads of things," John snapped back. He hated himself for never being able to find a great comeback when Nick verbally attacked.

"Yeah, he can paint as well as draw," Anna said, leaping to her friend's defense as the other boys all laughed. Chris gave him a double thumbs-up. He liked John's paintings.

"Not just art stuff though," John added, embarrassed. "I'm handy, I can build stuff. I put up those shelves in your bedroom."

Anna bit her lip at the memory of the shelves. She'd never told him how she'd had to redo the whole job after they'd collapsed on her head in the middle of the night.

"I killed a pig once," said Tibbsy. Everyone stopped and stared as he grinned back at them blankly.

"Awesome," Steph said, pushing through the group and leading the way through the darkened alley. "Because every apocalypse survival team needs its own sociopath." Tibbsy looked at Nick in hopes of a clue if that was a good thing or not.

One by one, the entire gang stopped outside a gaudily painted, ramshackle warehouse. Strings of tiny lights flashed on and off around a shoddily painted sign that read RUDOLPH'S CHRISTMAS TREE EMPORIUM—SALE NOW ON!

"It's Christmas Eve," Chris realized aloud. He smiled for a moment. Just for a moment.

"Could cut through here," Nick suggested to Anna as he nodded toward the dark and tightly packed lot of Christmas trees. "Quickest way to get to the school, find your dad." He looked back at his friends, all of them staring at him. "Plus it'll be fun, right lads?"

All four of them guffawed and leaped at one another in clumsy attempts at chest bumps.

"Yeah!" Steph pumped her fist in the air. "Certain death is so much fun!"

"Don't piss your pants," Nick scoffed, pushing her out of his way. "The men will keep the nasties away."

Graham, Jake, and Tibbsy assumed manly poses, grunting, while Steph naturally shifted her weight evenly across both feet. She quietly turned toward Nick, subtly raised her hand, and slapped him across the face once, hard. She rudimentarily assumed her place back in their informal lineup. No one moved. It was as if it never happened.

"It's pretty dark in there," Anna said, peering inside the warehouse. Nick was right. It was the quickest route, but there was no way to see what was inside.

"And it'll be dark outside soon as well," Nick reasoned, still a bit stunned. "We go this way, we might make it to the school before the sun goes down."

Anna looked back into the dark abyss of the warehouse and then back at Nick. There was an expression on his face that she'd seen only a few times before. He was being genuine for once. But still, it was a risk.

"Come on," he said, a half smile on his face. "You know we've got this."

John watched the two of them from a distance. How could she feel anything for that knob when she couldn't even bring herself to consider giving them a chance? He kicked at the ground as Nick sweet-talked her into getting exactly what he wanted. *And not for the first time,* John thought bitterly.

"All right," Anna said, almost relieved to let someone else make a decision for a moment. "Fun way it is."

Next to the doorway, she spotted a giant, novelty candy cane jammed in the dirt. With a determined yank, Anna pulled it out of the ground and tested the weight of it in her hands, noting its sharp, pointy end. It reminded her of a hockey stick, only far more festive, and she was fully aware of how much damage someone could do with a hockey stick. She hadn't played in years and still had bruises on her shins.

"Eh, can we vote on this please?" John asked, not exactly desperate to follow his rival to almost certain death.

"Live or die," Nick replied, resolute. "There's your vote."

Anna gave John a half smile before heading into the darkness with her candy-cane weapon in her hand. Nick followed closely behind, trailed by his goons, then Chris, and finally Steph. With a resigned sigh, John followed everyone inside.

"Right," Tony said, standing in front of the school doors with his keys in one hand and an ax in the other. "Everyone knows the plan, yes? Eyes open, stick together, and if you see something, say something. If we get separated, head toward the base. There's bound to be people waiting for us there, even if the soldiers outside . . . well. That's still the safest place to meet up, I reckon."

Murmurs moved through the crowd, everyone nodding and shaking, parents clutching small children's hands and trying not to cry.

At the back of the group, Lisa held on to Bea, one arm around her waist, the other holding her hand.

"Lisa, love," Bea whispered into her ear as Tony carried on giving his instructions.

Lisa chewed on the inside of her cheek, really not wanting to hear what she had to say.

"You've got to leave me here," she insisted. "I'll stay in one of the little offices until you can send help. I'll be fine."

"Chris wouldn't want me to leave you behind," Lisa replied, staring straight ahead. "We'll be all right if we stay together."

"No," Bea replied, quiet certainty in her weak voice. "I'm not going, love."

Lisa teared up and looked down at the fragile old woman. She was all the family Chris had and she just couldn't bear it.

"I'll stay with you," she offered. "We'll wait here until Chris comes to find us. I'm sure he's on his way."

"I'll wait here and you go and find him," Bea corrected. "You don't want to be stuck here with me when you should be out there with everyone else. I know you'll come back for me, love." She paused and smiled, pressing a papery hand against Lisa's cheek. "I'm not afraid."

"Let me talk to Tony," Lisa said, smothering the tears in her voice. "He'll know what to do."

As she turned to look for Anna's dad, a hand roughly shoved her out of the way, knocking her into Bea and sending them both flying into the wall.

"No!" Savage screamed, tearing through the gathered mass of people and heading straight for Tony. Everyone turned at once to look at him as he pressed his back against the front doors, blocking their exit. His face was beet red and there were flecks of spit in his beard. "No one is going anywhere!"

"Arthur, a decision has been made," Tony said as calmly as he could manage. He was through playing nice; Arthur wasn't listening anyway. The man didn't know the meaning of the word *reasonable*. "We're going to take our chances outside."

"No," Savage replied. His eyes were wide and bright behind his glasses, his arms stretched out wide like wings. "You're going to stay, you're going to listen to me. I'm sick of it, Shepherd, sick of all of you."

He shoved Tony out of his way and turned his vitriol on the cowering crowd.

"Look at you," he screamed. "Lambs trotting off to the slaughter. Idiot lambs. I should let you go, I should shake you all by the hand and send you out one by one, but I won't, I won't allow it. You're going to stay here, you're going to listen to me and you're going to do as you're told."

"You've lost it," Julie said, a grim look of determination on her face. "You always were an arsehole, Arthur, but this is going too far. You're not our leader, you're just a bully. What happened to you when you were a kid? Did you not get enough hugs from your mum and dad?"

"Don't you mention my parents!" he thundered, descending on her like a well-dressed scarecrow. "My parents were pillars of this community. They raised me properly, taught me manners, showed me wrong from right. They valued education and civility. Not like the foul beasts you allow to roam these halls day in and day out. Perhaps if you'd raised your children the way my parents raised me, we wouldn't be in this situation."

"You need to get out of our way," Julie warned, not afraid in the slightest. "Before I make you."

"And what are you going to do?" Arthur crooned, dancing around John's mother with wild spastic movements. "Draw a pretty picture of your feelings like your moron son?"

That was all it took. Julie drew back her hand and slapped Savage hard across the face, leaving a red imprint right above his beard on his pale cheek. His reaction was instantaneous.

"How dare you," he growled, grabbing the woman by the neck. Her eyes popped open as she tried to catch her breath. "How dare you speak to me this way? After everything I've done for the people of this town? After everything I've sacrificed for your idiot children!"

"Arthur, let her go!" Tony yelled, dropping his ax and grabbing at Savage's arms, but he was so much stronger than he would have guessed. "You're hurting her."

"And you're trying to kill her," Savage spat as Julie's eyes bugged out of her head, her hands clawing at his wrists. "Why don't we just open the doors and let those things in here? It'll be much more expedient, don't you think?"

"Let go, now!" Tony shouted.

Savage looked back at his victim as her eyes rolled backward and she went limp under his grip. Suddenly disgusted, he let go of her, pushing her away as hard as he could. Julie blinked and gasped for air, stumbling as she tripped backward, reaching her arms out into thin air. She seemed to be falling forever as Savage, Tony, and the rest of the assembled parents and children watched. And then, all at once, her head struck the sharp edge of the radiator and her body crumpled to the floor.

And then she was still.

"Arthur," Tony breathed without moving. "What have you done?"

"I didn't do anything," he replied. He stared down at Julie, her eyes already glassy, stuck wide open and staring back at him with unflinching accusation. "She fell. You saw it; she fell."

"Julie?" Tony collapsed to his knees and picked up her wrist. Her arm flopped lifelessly in his hand. "Oh God, Julie."

He looked up at Savage, a different kind of fear on his face.

"She's dead."

The parents gathered in the hallway took a collective breath, all of them moving backward, away from Arthur Savage, away from Tony Shepherd, and away from the dead body of Julie Wise.

"She slipped," Savage said slowly. "She fell."

"You *killed* her," Tony said, closing her eyes with tears running down his face. "And we all saw it."

"Yeah, we saw it!" An unseen person's voice broke out.

An accident, Savage told himself. *But was it?* the voice in his head whispered. *Was it really? Didn't she have it coming? Didn't they all have it coming?* A chorus of accusatory agreements echoed, rising in volume until he couldn't take it any longer.

"Shut up!" Savage screamed. "Shut up, all of you!"

The edges of Arthur's mouth twitched as he cast his eyes over the parents. He watched as they cowered, as they slunk away from him. They were afraid of him.

At last.

"I've had a change of heart," he said with a soft, calm smile. "Anyone who still wants to leave is more than welcome."

Not a single person moved. Everyone stared at Arthur Savage in utter horror. For the first time that day, they were much more afraid of what was inside the school than whatever might lie outside.

"No?" He freed his enormous ring of keys from his belt and pulled out the lock for the front door. "Are you sure?"

Slowly, deliberately, he slid the key into the lock.

"Arthur, no," Tony whispered, standing upright with Julie's body in his arms.

"But you were so keen to leave," Savage crooned.

With his gaze locked on Tony Shepherd, he squeezed the head of the key between his cold fingers and turned it sharply. The lock clicked and the door began to creak open, a blast of cold air shocking them all where they stood.

Arthur watched with a smile on his face as the parents caught their first glimpse of what awaited them outside. One by one, they all turned and ran back into the school, screaming.

"Now," he said softly, clipping his keys safely back into place. "Who wants to go first?"

20

"Yeah, this was a brilliant idea," John whispered to himself, bringing up the rear of the group. On any other Christmas Eve, he'd have been delighted to spend an hour or so screwing around in Rudolph's Christmas Tree Emporium with Anna and Chris, and what the hell, even Steph. She wasn't so bad when she wasn't trying to guilt trip him into sponsoring orphaned turtles in the Galapagos Islands. But this was not his idea of fun.

The warehouse was almost pitch-black and they were surrounded by row upon row of Christmas trees, all drying out for the want of a good watering, a shower of needles covering the floor every time he brushed past. And while he enjoyed the odd decorative elf as much as the next Christmas-obsessed seventeen-year-old male, in this situation they were just downright creepy. They peered out at them from every corner, making faces and grinning in their stupid green hats.

"I hate this plan," John muttered, hurrying to catch up to the others.

Anna felt him sidle up beside her and relaxed by a fraction. She just felt better when she knew where he was. It had always been that way.

"Anna," he whispered.

"Yeah?"

"Do you reckon my mom's okay?"

She bit her bottom lip and squinted into the dark.

"Of course," she replied. "Her and my dad."

"Big Tony's definitely all right," John said, treading carefully across the fallen branches. "He'll be telling everyone what's what. Your dad's one hundred percent A-okay, Anna."

"I hope so." Her voice cracked as she spoke. "He's all I've got."

"No, he isn't," John said, his hand finding hers in the dark. "You've got me and my mom, too. Always. We're family."

She smiled at her best friend, more grateful than ever to have him at her side.

✦ ✦ ✦

Chris held up his phone, filming as they moved slowly through the rows of Christmas trees. He glanced at the screen for just a second. Thirty percent battery left. Up ahead, Jake swung his own phone around, the flashlight in the front casting strange shadows. Long branches of prickly pine trees, stretching out monstrously against the corrugated steel walls.

With a sharp intake of breath, Chris raised his hand and everyone stopped dead in their tracks. He pointed at the closest mass of trees with his phone. There was something hiding inside the branches, something red. Holding her breath, Anna moved forward to investigate, only realizing Nick was right by her side when she squatted down to take a closer look. He prepared himself, readying his bat for action before nodding for Anna to act. Ignoring the stabbing pain of the pine needles, she wrenched the tree branches out of the way to reveal the interloper.

A brightly painted, creepy Mrs. Claus garden gnome with cherub cheeks. With an appearance similar to those of old baby dolls that lurk in the dusty clutter of an antiques store, the gnome's eyes lit up as it began to laugh a prerecorded laugh track, triggered by their movement.

Anna exhaled, looking up at Nick with a relieved smile. In the corner of her eye, she saw John's hurt expression and straightened her face. Chris turned and looked at everyone with a goofy grin.

"Guess there's nobody *gnome*."

One by one, everyone began to laugh, even Nick.

"Come on," Anna said, rolling her head from side to side to release some tension. "Let's get out of here."

All at once, the trees began to fall in on them, pots smashing and crashing against the ground, and sharp pine needles stabbing every inch of naked flesh. A zombie elf, his jolly green costume streaked with blackened blood, burst out of the trees and lurched at Anna. And he was not alone.

The gang screamed as more zombie elves appeared, arms stretching out of the pine trees, grabbing and scratching and clawing at the survivors.

"As if elves aren't already creepy enough!" Anna shouted in a panic. She reached out and grabbed John's wrist. Their eyes met and all was forgiven, she turned to run, her hand slipping over his as the trees shook and fell all around them. There were only a few more feet to go, she could see the back of the warehouse, the little room where you went to pay for your tree. *Just a few more steps,* she told herself, shutting out the chaotic screams and rumbling moans of the elves and when she looked back over her shoulder . . .

He was gone.

An elf leaped out in front of her, cutting off her route of escape and sending her back into the rows of trees. She was completely alone.

"John?" She called quietly at first, doubled over, panting for breath. "John! Guys! GUYS?!"

Nothing. No one. Just the echoing screams of her friends, somewhere out of sight. As terrified as she was, there was no way she was going to be eaten by zombie elves in Rudolph's Christmas Tree Emporium. She would impale herself on her candy cane before that happened. Without a clue what to do, she chose a direction and ran as fast as she could, her weapon swinging by her side. Skidding to a halt, Anna realized she'd hit a dead end. Before she could turn around and go back, she bumped straight into a bloodstained body. With a warrior's cry, she closed her eyes and brandished her candy cane, ready to fight to the death, but instead of hitting a zombie's skull, it crashed against something hard, something aluminum.

She opened one eye to see Nick holding out his baseball bat, a fresh wound on his forehead and a huge welt blooming under his right eye.

"You okay?" she asked, chest heaving with relief.

"I'm okay," he replied, looking back over his shoulder. "But we've got to keep going."

She nodded and they ran, side by side, not stopping until they hit a clearing littered with zombie body parts, Jake and Tibbsy doubled over in the middle of it all.

"Good work, you two," Nick said, kicking a savaged leg out of his way. "Come on, let's—"

"Nick!" Anna grabbed him and yanked him backward. Jake and Tibbsy weren't taking a celebratory breather. They were eating Graham.

"Aw, fuck." Nick's eyes opened saucer-wide. "They're my friends."

"They *were* your friends," Anna replied as Jake and Tibbsy turned, their faces covered in Graham's blood and guts. "Don't freeze on me, Nick."

But for the first time, he was lost. They inched closer, no hint of humanity in their eyes.

"J-Jake," he stuttered. "Tibbs?"

Behind them, slowly and shakily, Graham began to rise to his feet. All three had been turned. Nick raised his bat, preparing himself for the worst, but even as they crept closer and closer, he couldn't bring himself to do it.

"Move," Anna commanded, stepping in front of him and whacking Jake and Tibbsy with one heavy hit of her giant candy cane. As they staggered back into Graham, she took hold of Nick's hand and pulled him through another line of trees, pine needles scraping at their faces, until they emerged right next to the exit.

"Guys!" Steph hissed, waving to them from the open fire exit.

"C'mon," Nick said, hurling himself toward the door on very unsteady legs.

Anna, seeing Chris and his camera still in the tree lot, started after him.

"Wait!" She paused, turning to see nothing other than pine trees. "Where's John?"

Nick paused, steps away from the doorway.

"Come *on*, Anna!" he yelled, desperate to get out of there before his friends recovered and came for him again. He couldn't stand to see their faces transformed into something so hideous. Not that they'd been lookers in the first place, but still.

Anna shook her head.

"I'm going back for him. He wouldn't leave me behind."

"For fuck's sake," Nick muttered, taking a deep breath, ready to follow her back into the battleground just as John emerged, limping through the trees.

"What are you doing?" he asked, his face white and the tree on his sweater now covered in blood. "Move!"

Nick and Anna each grabbed an arm and yanked him out of the tree line, through the exit, and into the cold afternoon air.

Chris hovered by the doorway, filming the daring escape while Steph held the fire exit open.

"I've got some amazing footage," he shouted to Steph, waving his phone in the air as he jogged backward. "Wait until you see this!"

But then he tripped. As he struggled to keep himself upright, his phone slipped out of his hands and bounced on the ground, landing on the wrong side of the fire exit.

"NO!" Anna screamed as he immediately chased after it.

There was no way he was leaving it behind. All those pictures of him and Lisa, all the footage of the last twenty-four hours, not to mention he was at level three thousand on Candy Crush. He reached out to grab the phone just as Zombie Tibbsy hurled himself at his arm, snarling through the air, mouth open, teeth gnashing.

"Not today!" Steph appeared at Chris's side and punched the zombie in the head so hard, his jaw snapped and flew across the floor.

"You're on a liquid diet now," she said, helping Chris back up. "Stay off the red meat, it's bad for your cholesterol."

Nick held the door open until they were safely through, staring down his dead friends one last time before he slammed the door shut.

✦ ✦ ✦

"That was so stupid," Steph yelled at Chris, tears in her eyes and her hand throbbing.

"I know!" Chris yelled back.

He looked around, blinking at the boxes of running shoes and tennis rackets. They were in the sports shop. Before he could open his mouth to apologize, Steph barreled into him with a double-armed hug.

"Don't scare me like that again, okay, buddy?" she said, 100 percent definitely not crying. "It's just a phone—plastic and glass."

"And all my photos and videos," he replied, getting heated again. "Lisa and Gran are on here! I need it."

Seeing the fear in his eyes, Steph exhaled and tried a smile.

"They're alive, Chris," she said. "We'll find them."

But he was too scared to be reassured.

"You don't believe that!" he shouted as everyone turned to look. Anna didn't think she'd ever heard Chris raise his voice before. "You think everyone's dead. Your girlfriend, your parents. You don't even care!"

Steph stared back at him. Her face was completely blank, but there was fire in her eyes.

"You don't know me," she said quietly. "You don't know what I think."

Hurt, she turned her back and walked away, leaving Chris alone. Ashamed of his outburst, he squeezed his phone in his hand and kicked at a toppled mannequin. It didn't help.

✦ ✦ ✦

John limped over to a plastic chair next to the cash register. He watched as Nick and Anna came in together, Anna checking the door, then locking it behind her. He looked down at his blood-covered hands and sighed.

"I'm sorry about your friends," Anna said, raising her hand to comfort Nick.

He shrugged her off before she could even make contact.

"They should have kept up," he replied, dropping his bat on the floor and making a beeline for a display full of shiny new ones. Anna watched as he tested out each one, swinging it around and smashing assorted tennis balls into a wall of football shirts.

"Hey, how's the knee?" she asked, kneeling down beside John and straightening out his leg. Nick continued to test baseball bats and work through his grief by smashing up the store.

"Did you know his mates well?" John asked.

"Not really," Anna replied, picking her words carefully. She and John had never talked about what happened between her and Nick. He had been quite clear in letting her know he didn't approve.

Nick wasn't the only one working out his frustrations with weapons. Steph found a box of assorted mannequin limbs and tried swinging them around, one by one. Who needed a baseball bat when you could clobber zombies to death with a plastic shin?

"John?" Anna said, almost in a whisper. He looked down at his friend, kneeling on the floor at his side.

"What if everyone is dead?"

"Then you'll figure something out," he replied, trying very hard to be brave. "You usually do, Anna Shepherd. It's actually really annoying."

"What would I do without you?" she asked, trying on a little wry smile.

"Are we good to go?" Nick asked, his eyes completely void of emotion. "Or does John need to go and change his tampon?"

He pushed over a basket full of tennis balls and stalked toward the exit, Steph and Chris at his heels, armed with new weapons. A mannequin leg for Steph, and for some inexplicable reason, Chris had chosen a tennis racquet.

"I must admit." John winced as Anna helped him to his feet. "I can see why you found him so irresistible."

"Shut up," Anna ordered in a pleasant voice. "It's confirmed, I've got terrible taste in boys. Brilliant taste in best friends."

John smiled, hobbling along at her side.

"Oh, hey, do you want some genuine good news?" he asked. Anna quirked a disbelieving eyebrow. "I remember all the reindeer. You ready?"

She pushed open the shop door and took a deep breath as they emerged into the shopping center. It was too big, too open. They were far too exposed for Anna's liking.

"Dasher, Dancer, Comet, Vixen, Cupid . . ." John began listing Santa's reindeer with an enormous amount of pride in his voice.

"Cupid?" Anna questioned.

"I know, right?" John replied. "Who knew he was pulling double duty. So, Dasher, Dancer, Comet, Vixen, Cupid, Prancer, Donner, Blitzen, and Rudolph!"

He threw out his arms to deliver a jazz hands celebration, and as Anna opened her mouth to laugh, she saw it—the zombie hurtling toward him from behind.

The world went into slow motion. John waved his hand into range of its mouth, straight between its jaws, and Anna was powerless to stop it as the thing clamped down, tearing through John's flesh.

21

"No!" ANNA SCREAMED, even before John could realize what was happening. He didn't feel the bite at first, just the sensation of someone coming from behind him, and by then it was too late.

Everything went quiet for a moment.

Anna was battering the biter away from him, still screaming, tears running down her face as John looked down at his hand. He was still stuck to the spot when he saw the teeth marks, the blood, his own flesh hanging off the bone. He'd been bitten. The simple shock of it just wouldn't register, but deep down inside, he knew what happened next. He looked up at Anna, still pounding her candy cane into the skull of his attacker, screaming and screaming and screaming.

Until more of them appeared.

$\blacklozenge$ $\blacklozenge$ $\blacklozenge$

Nick, Chris, and Steph turned when they heard Anna's anguish.

Steph clapped her hand over her mouth when she realized what was happening. Anna and John were surrounded. There were literally dozens of zombies, from out of nowhere, circling their friends and creeping closer and closer. Nick scanned for a way to get Anna to safety, but the ring of zombies was impenetrable. He clutched his baseball bat so hard, he felt his skin burn against the grip, his mouth opening and closing, even though no words managed to find a way out.

They were trapped.

$\blacklozenge$ $\blacklozenge$ $\blacklozenge$

John was still staring at his wound. How was it possible? Yes, he'd seen people dying all day, but him, John Wise? He wasn't supposed to die. He was supposed to get to the school, find his mom and Anna's dad, and wait for the army to arrive, and then, when they were on the helicopter being transported over to some isolated base in Iceland or Greenland or some other country with "land" in its name, Anna would look at him and see him in a new way. Their eyes would meet and they'd need no words, and after all this, they would finally be together.

He wasn't supposed to die.

He looked up and saw the faces of the undead getting closer. The zombies that zeroed in around them weren't interested in him, they only wanted her. They already knew his life was down to mere moments. And if that was the case, he was going to make them count. Without a word, he grabbed hold of Anna Shepherd, the girl next door, pinning her arms to her side.

"What are you doing?" she wailed, kicking at the closest zombie, even as he picked her up off the ground.

"Saving the life of my best friend," he whispered into her hair.

He barged through the horde of zombies, hunching down and moving backward as though the room were on fire. And to John, it felt as though it was. His blood was already boiling, his flesh scorching on his bones. It had started. He wrapped his arms and torso protectively around Anna, protecting her with his own body, and plunged into the horde of biting zombies. As soon as he could force a gap in the ring that engulfed them, he spun on his heel, tossing Anna to safety. She tumbled to the floor at the feet of her friends, candy cane still in her hand. She looked up, just in time to meet his brown eyes as they faded away to gray.

"John!" she screamed, losing control of absolutely all that she was. "No!"

He fell back, swallowed by the horde as they punished him for saving her.

"Leave it!" Nick yelled, grabbing one of her arms to try to hold her back. Steph grabbed the other, but they were fighting a strength that not even Anna knew she had in her.

"He's gone!"

Unable to break their grip, she turned into Nick's chest, punching him over and over as he tried to comfort her. Chris and Steph didn't know what to do. Chris just stared into space in disbelief. Pretending the zombies weren't feasting on their friend felt like a disservice to John, but watching them pull him apart was just sick. Chris vomited.

Across the shopping center, Nick saw more coming. He nudged Steph, pointing to the coming invasion.

"Hey." Steph turned back to Anna, her angry punches now nothing more than hollow sobs. "Hey, we have to go, can you hear me?"

Anna shook her head. She couldn't leave him. She couldn't bear it.

"Your dad is waiting," Steph reminded her, grabbing her chin in her hand and looking her straight in the eye. "We have to get to your dad, right?"

Sucking in her breath, Anna blinked at her friend

with wild eyes. She managed a nod, even if she didn't fully understand what she was saying.

"That's it," Steph said, leading them all away and out toward the glowing green exit sign. Chris kept up the back while Nick wrapped an arm around Anna, half carrying her as she dragged herself away.

"He wanted you to get out of here, Anna, that's what we're gonna do."

"Um, Steph?" Chris said, skipping up to the front. "I think what we might want to do is run."

She turned around and gasped. The gaggle of zombies had swarmed into an army.

"Okay, change of plan," she wailed. "Anna, look alive. I'm gonna need that fighting spirit of yours to get through this."

With one last choked sob, Anna tightened her grip on the candy cane and pushed herself away from Nick's arms. Swiping at her dirty, tear-stained face with the sleeve of her shirt, she swung her candy cane up onto her shoulder. The next thing that came within ten feet of her was going to pay for this.

✦ ✦ ✦

Vengeance was swift but severe. Anna, Nick, Chris, and Steph started kicking and swiping and stabbing at anything that got in their way. It was a bloodbath but it wasn't their blood that was being spilled. For the first time, the zombies began to back away from the humans, but Anna wasn't about to let them get away that easily.

Chris ran alongside Anna, determined to protect her the way John would have wanted, but in reality it was Anna doing most of the protecting. Every time he stumbled, he forced himself up. Steph had been right, he had to try for his gran's sake and for Lisa's. If Nick and his friends had survived the night, there was no reason they couldn't be safely tucked away somewhere. Turning swiftly, he thwacked a little girl zombie in the face as he ran.

Steph channeled every thought of government and corporate injustice she had fought over the last few years into the same determination as the rest of them, and she had something else. The will to survive and a mannequin leg. Maybe they were still alive for a reason, she thought as she drove the studded end of the leg through a zombie shop assistant's forehead. John certainly hadn't sacrificed himself so that they could fall down and die in front of a tuxedo rental joint. She had no idea what they'd discover at that school, but she was sure as shit going to get there to find out.

Nick reached out an arm to help Steph up as she stumbled over an abandoned suitcase. He gave her a tense smile before grimly battling on, one eye on Anna, the other on the attacks that came at them from every angle. It had been the worst day of his entire life, the worst day of most people's lives, he had to guess. First his dad, then his friends, and then John? They weren't about to sit down and braid friendship bracelets for each other, but that was brutal. And brave. He'd been a true hero. Now it was up to Nick to see it through.

No such thoughts ran through Anna's head. She punched and she kicked and she fought with every ounce of strength in her body. All she saw was the look on John's face before they dragged him into their midst. The love in his eyes as he watched her friends pull her to safety. Ahead, a pantomime horse swayed toward them, clearly operated by the undead.

Chris gasped.

Anna growled.

Nick attacked first, clubbing the front of the horse with his bat, while Steph and Chris took it in turns to batter the back half. With a primal scream, Anna charged, stabbing it over and over until it stopped fighting back.

"I think it's done," Steph said, dragging her off the top of the horse.

"Yeah," Chris said, kicking the back end just to make sure. "No point beating a dead horse." *That pun was for you, John*, he thought.

"We're not finished yet," Nick said, pointing at the

last obstacle standing between them and the exit. Zombie Santa Claus. "If we all get out of here alive, the first round is on me."

"*When* we all get out of here alive," Anna corrected, charging straight at the deranged Santa. "Mine's a rum and Coke."

"I'll take a Jack Daniel's, neat," Steph replied, following close behind.

Chris paused, giving Nick a questioning look.

"What?" he asked as the girls smashed straight into St. Nick, beating it down to its knees.

"I don't like alcohol," Chris said. "Can I have an ice cream instead?"

"Sure," Nick agreed sarcastically as they chased after Anna and Steph. "Full banana split with a cherry on top."

"Brilliant." Chris grimaced as he drove the handle of his tennis racket through Father Christmas's forehead. "Then you're on."

22

It was dark by the time they reached the school, all four of them bloody, battered, and exhausted. But they had made it. Anna couldn't quite believe it, completely on edge as they stood in front of the main entrance. Was it really only two days since she stood in that exact same spot, arguing with her dad? Didn't seem possible.

"It's too quiet," she said, eyeing the boards nailed to the inside of the windows. Nick slowly pushed at the door with one finger. It was unlocked.

"And I hate to say it, but that's not a good sign," Nick agreed as the door creaked rustily on its hinges. "Everyone needs to be on guard, okay?"

Anna nodded. Chris and Steph said nothing.

What if her dad wasn't here, after everything they'd been through? Anna thought, following Nick up the front steps. Or even worse, what if he was here but he wasn't her dad anymore. . . .

"On my mark." Nick held up a closed fist and the others waited, desperate to know what was on the other side of the door. Anna took hold of one door, Nick took the other. On her nod, Nick lowered his fist and they pulled the doors open together, all four of them charging inside at once.

✦ ✦ ✦

Anna thought she was prepared for almost anything: a massacre, her dad turned into a zombie, even an empty, post-evacuation school. She'd run through every possible scenario in her head on the way over, but she had not been ready for this.

Behind the glass partition that separated the school reception from the office, Assistant Principal Savage was sitting in the school's secretary's chair, humming along to Christmas carols while he scarfed a cooked turkey dinner from a paper plate.

He looked up at the four students, Chris, hanging on to Steph for dear life, Nick, brandishing his baseball bat, and Anna, of course it was Anna, standing in front, bloody and bruised but still very much alive. Savage swallowed a particularly dry piece of turkey and took a sip of wine before greeting them with a smile.

"What . . . are . . . you . . . doing?" Steph asked. It was a tough call but she had to admit, this was probably the weirdest thing she'd seen all day.

Savage dabbed at the side of his mouth with a freshly starched napkin, straightened his tie, and stood up.

"I'm having my Christmas dinner, Miss North," he replied, as if it was the most perfectly normal thing in the world. "Ah, Miss Shepherd. I see you're still with us. Suppose you'll all be wanting to see your parents. You're lucky, they almost left without you."

Anna's eyes widened at the mention of the word "parents." Her dad was alive. Excitedly, she followed Savage down the hallway to a locked door. He beckoned for the others to follow, and Chris bounded after them like a happy puppy.

"Something's wrong," Nick whispered to Steph. "He's never this nice."

They already knew *their* parents weren't inside, and neither of them trusted this new, reasonable Mr. Savage.

"Maybe the end of the world brought out his good side," she suggested, following Chris, Anna, and the assistant principal cautiously.

"Hell on Earth couldn't make this guy civil," Nick said, shaking his head. "I don't like it."

"In you go," Savage said with a smile, opening the

door to the cafeteria with a flourish. "So glad you were able to join us in time for dinner."

Anna and Chris rushed inside with Nick and Steph following. Steph flashed Savage a look as she passed, but he just smiled down at her, a happy twinkle in his blue eyes.

"Merry Christmas," he whispered as he closed the door behind them.

✦ ✦ ✦

It was dark in the cafeteria, nothing but little strings of battery-powered Christmas lights picking out spots of brightness in the pitch-black. Anna blinked, waiting for her eyes to adjust, searching the seemingly empty room for her dad. Suddenly, the Christmas music they'd heard in reception began playing through the cafeteria speakers and they saw someone move at the back of the room. It was the parents, surrounding a table and far too preoccupied to notice the newcomers.

"What the . . ." Steph breathed as Savage appeared on the other side of a metal-shuttered service window where the hair-netted cafeteria workers usually served food. He had a manic grin on his face as he raced to the next one and pulled down the last mesh guard between them. She reached out to try the door they'd entered through, but it was locked. There was no way out. Savage looked at her and shrugged happily. One by one, the parents turned to face them, and Steph saw what was on the table.

It was John's mom, Julie, her guts spilling out from the inside and smeared all over the hands and faces of her friends.

They'd been turned, every single one of them.

Behind the serving hatch, Savage flicked the switch on a little portable lamp, illuminating a fresh plate of turkey and all the trimmings. Anna felt her legs go weak and reached for the wall to steady herself. Forcing herself to look, she searched for her dad but he wasn't there. She didn't know whether to be thankful or not.

"What the *fuck*?" Steph finally finished her sentence, her stomach churning at the scene in front of her.

"You know, Miss North," Savage said, tucking in to a roasted potato. "For such a serious journalist as yourself, your vocabulary leaves a lot to be desired."

"He's gone full Britney," Steph muttered. "Shaved head, 2007, umbrella-wielding Britney."

Inside the kitchen, Savage giggled and spun around on his office chair.

Chris leaned across to whisper to Anna, unable to take his eyes off the macabre scene at the other end of the room.

"I don't see Lisa," he said, voice thick with the same fear and relief she felt. "Or my gran."

"My dad isn't here, either," Anna replied, shaking. "But I think that's John's mom on the table. . . ."

Savage leaned forward, pressing against the mesh divider to follow their gaze.

"Oh yes," he said, sitting back down and tucking his napkin into his collar. "It turns out if you kill people before they're bitten, they don't come back as zombies. Interesting, isn't it?"

He crunched a Brussels sprout, still grinning.

It took Anna a moment to understand what he was saying and it was a moment too long. Savage's noisy crunching was beginning to attract the attention of the former parents.

"You killed Julie?" she breathed.

"Accidents happen," Savage replied casually, chomping away. "Where's that boy of hers? Seems as though he is always following you around like a puppy that needs to be put down."

Anna's heart ached at the very mention of John.

"Ahh." Savage paused, took a sip of wine, and then continued. "From the look on your face, someone already took care of that part."

"Shut up," she whispered.

"Anna, stay calm," Nick whispered, eyes still fixed on

the horror in front of him. He had to get them out of there; his dad would expect him to get them out of there, but there was no escape route. No windows, no fire exits. The only way out was through the kitchen and Psycho Savage had taken care of that.

"Tell me," Savage said, leaning forward once again. "Did you see it happen? Did you even try to help him?"

"You're a teacher, for God's sake," Anna replied, vibrating with rage. "What is wrong with you?"

"Not so cocky now, are we, Miss Shepherd?" His little smile turned into a wide, teeth-baring grin. Savage raised his shiny silver whistle to his lips before lowering his voice to a hateful whisper. "I can't wait to show your dad what's left of you."

"NO!" Steph yelled as he blew the whistle hard. The shrill, high-pitched sound grabbed the zombies' attention and they turned toward the light. Behind the mesh guard, Savaged pointed to the four students, nothing in his eyes but complete and utter insanity.

"Where's my dad?" Anna yelled as the zombies charged.

"Anna, on your left!" Nick shouted, swiping at Jake's dad with his baseball bat. Anna looked up to see the local milkman bearing down on her with considerably more speed than he managed in his milk deliveries. She pulled back her candy cane and hammered him through the neck.

"You little shits!" Savage barked, clawing at the mesh guard like an animal. "You should have listened to me, you should have all listened to me!"

"What a fantastic time for a psychotic meltdown," Steph barked, kicking some random kid's mom in the face. "You couldn't have lost it during spring break?'

"No time for wisecracks now, Miss North," he replied as he spun around in his chair. "You foul little gits had this coming. You think you're so important, that everyone ought to listen to every thought that goes through your vacuous heads. Well, guess what? No one cares anymore! You're a wasted generation. I've always known it and now it's time for the cull!"

"You sick bastard!" Steph grabbed the handle of the door one more time, rattling it with all her might as Chris delivered his best forehand on his next-door neighbor with his tennis racquet. It was no use, he'd locked it from the outside and there was no way to break the door down.

"Up here!" Nick yelled from on top of a table. Chris and Anna clambered up beside him, looking for an escape route, but Steph tripped, rolling straight into the barrier between Savage and the zombies.

"I've been biting my tongue forever," he hissed, pressing

his face up alongside her own. Steph winced, not certain as to which was worse—Savage's breath or being peed on by an undead nana. "And now retribution is here. They say youth is wasted on the young, don't they, Miss North? At least you won't be a waste; more like a nutritious meal."

Steph struck the barrier with her fist, but he pulled back, dodging her blow with a cackle and picking up his wine, safe in his tiny prison. He smiled as a zombie reached down and grabbed Steph's face with a bloody hand. She screamed, swiping with her mannequin leg, kicking, punching, anything to get it off her, but it was so strong, too strong. A chair flew through the air, toppling the zombie. Steph looked up to see Anna holding out a hand, ready to pull her to her feet.

But saving Steph had been a risky maneuver. All four of them pressed their backs against the mesh guard, Savage behind them, zombies in front. It was impossible to say which was a more dangerous situation.

"Hey, kids." Savage marched up and down the line, crowing into their ears. "School's not boring anymore, is it? I've been calling you zombies for years. Looks like I was right!"

"The only way out is through the kitchen," Nick said as all four fought off zombie after zombie after zombie. They were relentless, and Anna was already so tired.

They couldn't keep this up forever. "We have to try to break the screen down."

"Agreed," Anna said with a firm nod. While Steph and Chris kept the undead threat at bay, Anna and Nick hurled themselves at the mesh partition, throwing their entire weight at it over and over. But nothing happened.

"Good try," Savage called from inside. "More initiative than I'd have expected from you, Miss Shepherd. I'll be sure to mention that to your father when I deliver the bad news."

That was when Anna noticed the lock. The barrier was only held down by a small padlock, a tiny thing, almost like the kind of lock she'd put on her diary when she was a little girl. And most importantly, it was on their side of the barrier.

"Nick, keep them off us," she commanded, wedging the pointy end of her candy cane into the padlock. Savage peered closer at what she was doing, the smile on his face faltering for a second.

"Give up, Miss Shepherd," he said, waving his key ring at her. "You're only delaying the inevitable. The kindest thing would be to end your friends' suffering before you all end up meeting the same end. I have to tell you, it doesn't look like a pleasant way to go."

Ignoring the psychopath in the kitchen, Anna strained against her candy cane, screaming as she pushed the blade down on the lock with every ounce of energy left in her. And then, it popped open.

Savage blinked in shock as the lock fell to the floor with a clink. Anna looked at Nick, turned to kick the village postmaster in the balls, and then pushed up the barrier, dragging Nick, Chris, and Steph through to the other side.

23

"WHERE'S MY DAD?" Anna screamed as the sound of Savage's footsteps echoed through the kitchen. He was gone before they'd even hit the floor.

"The barrier!" Chris wailed as zombie hands began to creep over the counter. Steph grabbed the mesh guard and hauled it down, chopping off fingers and leaving bloody stumps littered all over Savage's cooking.

"Still more appetizing than anything that man cooked," she said, jamming a knife through the guard to keep the guard down and the furious undead on the other side of the mesh. "We'll get my car keys from his office," she said, pointing at herself and Chris. "You guys go find your dad and we'll meet outside."

Anna nodded and ran off, adrenaline pushing her on.

"I'm with you," Nick said, suddenly at her side.

She nodded but didn't say anything. The only thing that mattered now was finding her dad and getting the hell out of there.

The first open door they found led them into the workshop. It looked the same as it always did: dusty, gloomy, and not somewhere Anna wanted to be.

"He must have come through here," Anna said as they prowled through the room, checking underneath the benches. "All the other doors were locked."

Nick didn't reply. He stopped in front of a bench and traced his fingers along the surface. His own name was carved into the wood, along with three others. JAKE, TIBBSY, GRAHAM. He stared at the letters, remembering the day he carved them with his compass. They were supposed to be making bird boxes, but who cared about birds? No one now, that was for sure. If there even were any birds after all this was over.

"Nick?"

He looked up to see Anna, still wielding her candy cane.

"Yeah," he said, wiping his face with his sleeve and snapping back to attention. "You got something?"

"He's not here." She kicked a box full of wood shavings. "He must have gone the other way, just forgot to lock this room."

"Or unlocked it to trick us," he suggested. "We'll get

the crazy bastard, don't worry. We're the dream team, me and you."

Anna let out a deep breath.

"We might be a lot of things, Nick," she said, combing her hands through her knotted hair. "But we've never been a team."

She headed for the door, frustrated and exhausted and ready for all this to be over.

"It wasn't me, you know," Nick called, stopping her in her tracks. "After you stayed at my place. I didn't say nothing to no one."

Anna turned back to look him in the eye.

"Wait, you think that's why I'm angry with you?" she asked, incredulous at the forced innocence on his face.

"Well, obviously," he answered.

"Nick, I don't care about the sex and who knows about it," Anna said, finally saying the words out loud. "I'm angry with you because we shared all that stuff about our dads, and our future, and you acted like it meant something. Then you just ignored me. I opened up and trusted you and you just used me."

"Oh," Nick replied, looking oddly relieved. "Right."

"That's it?" She couldn't believe him. But still, it was strangely pleasant to still be surprised by someone's behavior after the forty-eight hours she'd had. "You're such a prick."

She turned to leave, no longer concerned whether he was with her or not.

"Just because your little fuck buddy died, don't go taking it out on—"

But Anna didn't give him a chance to finish his sentence.

"Don't you dare talk about my best friend like that!" she roared, shoving him backward against a bench. "He sacrificed his life for us. What have you ever done that wasn't just about yourself?"

Nick stuck out his chin, defiant, staring her down where she stood.

"Killed my dad," he said.

Anna took a step back. It would be a terrible thing to lie about.

"He got bit," Nick slowly explained, his bottom lip beginning to tremble as he spoke. "So he gave me his bat, told me not to let him down, told me to do the right thing for once in my life. So I did . . ."

His voice broke as he sank down onto one of the benches, pinching the bridge of his nose as his eyes burned with tears he didn't know he still had.

"Jesus."

Anna sank down beside him, not quite touching him, but not pulling away either. Nick sucked in one sharp, single breath and set his shoulders.

"Right," he said, standing up and fixing his gaze into the distance. "Enough pansy bollocks."

She stood quietly. There was nothing she could say that would make this better. They'd work it out in time, she thought. If they had enough time.

Nick opened the door to the hallway, but they were no longer alone.

"Shit," he whispered.

Anna pushed him out of the way to see dozens of zombies filling the hallway from both directions.

They were trapped.

✦ ✦ ✦

Upstairs, Steph and Chris crept through the corridor in silence. Every time Steph started to say something funny to break the tension, she saw another bloody handprint on the wall, another torn poster covered in red smears.

"I didn't mean it before," Chris said, noticing as she stared at a shredded periodic table. "About your parents and stuff."

"It's okay, I know what I'm like." Steph shrugged, moving onward. "People love to tell me. I'm 'difficult.'"

"I think you're all right," he replied. "And whatever happens, you've got us now."

There was no forced earnestness or saccharine bullshit in his voice, just classic Chris honesty. A half smile found

223

its way onto her face. In the midst of all this horror, it was nice to finally have a friend.

"Can you hear that?" Steph whispered, standing still and holding her breath. It was faint, so faint, but she was almost sure she could hear music. "You think it's Savage?"

"No," Chris replied, his eyes opening wide. "That's Lisa's favorite song. She's got to be up here."

He took off down the corridor, following the music and pressing his ear against every door. Eventually he stopped outside a storage closet. Steph held on to his arm, just to let him know she was there. She wanted to tell him it was going to be okay, but she couldn't. And she knew if Lisa had been turned, she was going to have to be the one to take care of her. It was what a friend would do.

Chris grabbed the door and yanked it open. His gran lay on the floor, unmoving, while Lisa was hunched over her in a little ball. He reeled backward, so ready to believe the worst, when Lisa turned to face him.

"Chris?" she whispered.

Gasping with joy, he collapsed to his knees, bundling her up in a tight hug, smelling her hair, kissing her head as Steph pushed him inside the closet and closed the door behind him, standing sentry.

"I can't believe it's really you," Lisa said through choking sobs. "I thought . . . perhaps . . . you . . ."

He broke away from their hug, finally turning attention to his gran. Lisa was still crying heavy, wracking sobs, and he realized they weren't tears of joy.

"I'm so, so sorry," she choked out as Chris looked down at his grandmother. Eyes closed, a smile on her face. She looked so peaceful. "We were going to leave, Anna's dad wanted to go out to find Anna, but then Savage opened the doors. We had to run and when we got here her heart just . . . She laid down and then she was gone, just like that. I'm sorry, baby."

Steph bit her lip, meeting Lisa's eyes with as much sympathy as a human being could possibly muster. She couldn't even imagine what that girl had been going through. Lisa gave her a tiny smile in return.

"At least she's not one of them," Chris said bravely, laying a hand on his grandmother's shoulder. It felt too strange to see her so still. She'd always been so excitable, so full of life. Always the first on the dance floor at a party, even with her heart condition. His family used to joke that she'd outlive all of them, and he'd never even questioned it. After everything they'd seen today, how could she just be gone?

"I don't want to be the one to say it, but we've got to go," Steph said, keeping an eye on the hallway. "They're bound to find their way up here eventually."

Lisa nodded in agreement before unsnapping a hair-clip from her own hair and sliding it into Bea's. A final parting gift. Chris leaned down and kissed her forehead.

"Bye, Gran," he said as he rose to his feet, stepped into the hallway, and closed the door behind him.

24

THE UNDEAD MOB outside the workshop was growing deeper by the second. Anna and Nick pushed against the door, trying to shut them out, but it was no good. There were too many of them. With one surge, they forced the door open, sending Anna and Nick flying.

"You've got to get out of here," Nick said, warming up his batting arm. "I'll hold them back."

"No way," Anna replied as she steeled herself for another battle. "We stick together."

He opened his mouth to speak, but she cut him off with a sharp look.

"You're hard work," he muttered.

"I've heard that before," she said, smiling a little at the thought of it. "And don't speak too soon. We're not done for yet."

Pulling back her candy cane, Anna prepared to charge, but instead she suddenly felt Nick push her backward, away from the fray.

"Come on, then!" he screamed, bashing skulls left and right. "Show me what you've got."

"Nick!" Anna screamed as they all turned their attention on him. "What are you doing?"

But it was clear what he was doing. Slowly but surely, he led the throng of zombies toward the back of the workshop, luring them through a maze of desks and workbenches. Away from Anna. For a fleeting moment, she saw an escape route.

"Don't just stand there like a dick!" Nick yelled. "Get out!"

"For fuck's sake," she choked. Was she really going to have to leave another friend to this fate?

"I want you to get your dad," he shouted, climbing up onto one of the workbenches before kicking a zombie geography teacher's head clean off his shoulders. He'd never liked geography. "Please, just go."

She nodded at the determination in his eyes as he swung the bat down onto the French teacher Mademoiselle Rouselle's skull. Without looking back, she darted around the gaggle of undead educators and out the front door.

"Close it!" Nick ordered from on top of his workbench. His eyes flickered down for just a second. NICK, JAKE, TIBBSY, GRAHAM. They were right there with him. "I've got this!"

And as the zombies swarmed forward, Anna did as he asked. Choking back tears as she ran, she heard Nick psych himself up with his anthem: *"When it comes to killing zombies, I'm the top of my class. While you've been hiding, I'll be kicking some ass . . ."*

✦ ✦ ✦

The staff room at Little Haven High School was a depressing place to be, even when there wasn't a zombie apocalypse. Steph peered through the window in the door, to see their teachers shambling around, clutching moldy coffee cups and stumbling on the frayed carpet.

"I can't tell," she muttered. "You think they've been turned or not?"

"Far too hard to tell," Chris replied, watching them bump into one another and groan nonsensically. "Let's assume yes?"

"Seems like a safe bet." Lisa nodded. "Where are your keys?"

Steph pointed toward a door on the other side of the room that bore the plaque MR. SAVAGE'S OFFICE.

"He's always taking my stuff from me. I spend more time in there than I do in class," she replied. "You two stay here, I know exactly where he keeps them."

"No!" Chris began to protest, but she had already slipped inside the staff room and closed the door on her friend.

"I've got this," she mouthed through the window as Chris and Lisa pressed themselves up against the glass.

It was cold inside. The heating had clearly been off for a while, and the air in front of Steph's mouth fogged up when she breathed out. She looked around at the other people in the room. No breath, no fog. Definitely zombies. She crouched down low, staying out of their sight lines. Sure, they were violent, flesh-eating monsters, but they weren't all that smart. If they didn't see you, they didn't attack you. *Like the T-Rex in* Jurassic Park, she reasoned as she crawled across the disgusting carpet, *only with slightly more proportional arms.*

Holding back behind a padded chair, she steadied herself, preparing to make the final sprint into the office. Something that used to be her media studies teacher, Miss Wright, limped by, leaving the path clear.

"Let's do this," she whispered, propelling herself forward. But before she could make it through the door, the zombie turned and stopped right in front of her. Steph's nose was literally an inch from its moldering shins. She closed her eyes and tried not to panic. *If it looks down I'm toast.* Too many thoughts crowded her mind as she crouched on the ground. Her parents, her girlfriend. All the things she wanted to say to them, all the *sorrys* and *thank yous* she owed. She tried to imagine herself on the edge of the lake at her folks' cottage, drinking a cocktail and wearing that polka-dot two-piece her mom bought her that she hated, with Veronica by her side. That's where she would be, she thought with an almost-smile, if she could be anywhere.

Outside in the hallway, Chris grabbed the door handle, ready to rush to Steph's aid. He was not about to let her go out all alone, but Lisa stopped him just in time.

"Wait!" she said, grabbing his arms and pointing toward the ceiling of the staff room. "Look."

The zombie that had stopped right in front of her wasn't looking down. It was looking up, eyes fixated on a piece of tinsel hanging from the ceiling. A shaft of light from the flickering fluorescent tubes in the hallway made it sparkle as it turned this way and that. The zombie smiled.

Steph didn't need anyone to tell her what to do. Not wasting another single second, she crawled onward and slid inside Savage's office, closing the door as quietly as possible.

The office was so utterly Arthur Savage, Steph could hardly stand to be in there. There were framed photos on the wall, no friends or family, but Savage shaking hands with the mayor, standing two over from a former prime minister, a very old picture of him appearing on *University Challenge*.

"Tragic," she muttered, ignoring the faded "Be a Winner" poster with its curling edges and moving straight over to the shelf marked CONFISCATED. Every single item he had gleefully taken from students was lined up and displayed like a trophy. Steph grabbed a satchel from the floor and filled it with Savage's precious things: spare phones, a flashlight, a chisel. But no keys. She delved into a box of random treasures at the end of the shelf, fishing through earrings, sunglasses, iPods, and—

"Urgh!"

She pulled her hand out and immediately dropped a huge pink vibrator.

"I hate this school," Steph said, gagging as she attempted to turn off the buzzing piece of pink rubber. "Uh, sorry, St. Peter," she whispered, fighting with the ON/OFF button. "But I was trying to save my friends' lives and instead I accidentally switched on a huge vibrating dildo and dropped it on the floor and then I got eaten by zombies. May I come in?"

Her keys weren't on the shelf or in the box. Unless

he had them with him, there was only one other place he could have hidden them. The little locked door in his desk. But without the keys . . .

"This calls for a little well-timed vandalism," she said with a smirk, grabbing the chisel from her new bag of tricks.

✦ ✦ ✦

Steph was so focused on the task at hand, she didn't even think to look back through the blinds, and it was just as well. The sound of the dildo had gotten the attention of several zombies when they heard the sound of something hitting the floor in the office.

"Uh-oh," Chris said, biting his thumbnail as they started toward the corner of the room.

The zombie teachers were swarming, just waiting for her to open the door. The moment she did, she was dead meat, literally.

"We've got to distract them," Chris said, stepping into the staff room before Lisa could stop him.

"Try the tinsel," she suggested, following close behind. "They like that."

"Here, zombies!" Chris called softly, shaking a sad strand of balding tinsel in the general direction of the undead. But it did nothing. Steph's brains were far more interesting to them than Christmas decorations.

"I know," Chris said with a triumphant smile, edging toward the TV. "Let's see what's on telly . . ."

✦ ✦ ✦

With one muted crunch, Steph forced her way into the desk drawer, the lock dropping onto the threadbare carpet with a dull thud. Inside were his most precious, private possessions. A well-thumbed self-help book titled *Victim to Victor*, a black-and-white photograph of what looked like the world's most depressed married couple to have ever existed, and a thank-you card. Steph wrinkled her nose at the faded drawing on the front; it looked ancient. The spine was gray and cracked, and inside it read, HAVE A GRATE SUMMER, MR. SAVAGE. REBECCA, 2D.

"I guess you weren't always an evil, homicidal monster," she whispered before dropping it back into the drawer with a shrug. She contorted her arm, twisting against the join to shove her forearm way up inside the desk, fumbling around until the tips of her fingers found something metallic. Her car keys!

"Yes!" she gasped, snatching them up as something like hope surged through her for the first time. Until she heard the laughter coming from the staff room.

Peering through the blinds, she saw the TV playing in the far corner, every single one of the zombies fixated on the bright colors and happy sounds. She followed a cable running out the back of the TV to a phone, held in a small, pale human hand.

Not a single channel was still airing when Chris turned on the TV, confirmation as far as he was concerned that this truly was the end of civilization. But he still had one trick up his sleeve. He connected his phone to the television and turned on his videos. Lisa rehearsing for the Christmas show, Anna and John messing around on the playground, and then, Steph reporting from the soup kitchen. The zombie Miss Wright seemed much more interested in the new version of his show reel, he noted with misplaced pride as the zombies moved away from Savage's door and began to gather around the glowing screen. Steph had a clear route out from the office to the hallway.

He reached down and felt for Lisa's hand as he raised his head over the parapet of the television, before ducking right back down, not sure what to say.

The zombies had them surrounded.

25

"WHAT ARE YOU doing?" Steph mouthed, her heart sinking as she emerged from the office to see Chris and Lisa staring helplessly at her from behind the television.

Chris shrugged as silent tears began to fall down Lisa's cheeks. He squeezed her hand tightly, determined to protect her, to protect everyone. He just wanted to be brave, like John. But he also wanted to be alive, which was not like John.

"Crawl!" Steph hissed, doing her best to mime the movement. "I got the keys!"

"We can do this, boyfriend," Lisa whispered into his ear before planting a sweet kiss on his cheek. He smiled at her encouraging face and nodded to her, to himself, and to Steph. They carefully got on all fours and moved slowly across the carpet. They were both going to be absolutely fine.

Over their heads, he could hear the videos playing. He could hear John laughing and joking, Lisa singing at the top of her lungs. Happy, loud, joyful sounds that he had almost forgotten.

Steph fidgeted in silence, pressing the sharp edge of her car keys into her thumb to keep herself focused. They were so close, crawling through the mob of zombies staring mindlessly at the TV screen. Lisa froze as she brushed the leg of her tenth-grade math teacher, but he was far too invested in a clip of Anna hurling balls from the ball pit at John's face to notice. Breathing out, she began to crawl again. Steph grinned, giving them a thumbs-up as they pushed closer and closer and closer . . . until the videos on the TV suddenly cut out.

On the floor, Chris's phone flashed with a low battery warning.

As the screen faded to black, the zombies blinked at one another before slowly, so slowly, turning to see Chris and Lisa crawling through their legs. The furious roar that followed shook Steph's bones. She fished around in her bag for the chisel, wishing she still had her mannequin leg as the undead attacked.

Jamming the tool straight into the eye socket of the

nearest teacher, she watched as Chris and Lisa scrambled away. In the wrong direction.

"Get out!" she yelled, jabbing indiscriminately as the zombies kept coming, but neither of them seemed to know what to do.

Chris scampered backward, pushing himself against the wall as Miss Wright approached. He winced at what was left of her face, turning away as she came closer with her teeth bared. He'd always secretly thought Miss Wright was attractive, but that was no longer the case. He definitely preferred her with skin, rather than without.

"Please," he whimpered, trying to reason with whatever might be left of her. "Please don't."

It was pointless. Miss Wright wasn't there.

But Lisa was.

"Get away from him!" she wailed, grabbing the teacher by the neck and hurling her across the room. Their eyes met for a brief moment, a smile on both of their faces. And then Lisa screamed.

"No!" Chris cried out, catching his girlfriend as she fell into his arms, the zombie still chomping on her shoulder. He lashed out without thinking, punching it away, knocking its nose right off its face, but the second he turned away, Miss Wright took her chance. She grabbed hold of his arm and tore into his flesh.

"Chris!"

Steph felt the bite almost as if it had happened to her. They were both bitten, Lisa and Chris. *After all they went through to find each other, they don't deserve this*, she thought, still battling her second-period chemistry teacher, eventually jabbing him through the throat with her chisel.

Chris and Lisa stared at each other's wounds in disbelief as the zombies turned away from them, all their attention on Steph.

"We can't let them get her," Lisa gasped, pressing her hand against the stinging bite on her shoulder. It was already starting to burn. Chris nodded. He knew what he had to do. Pushing through the crowd of snapping jaws, no danger to him now, he canceled the power save on his phone. There was ten percent left in the battery. Enough time for Steph to escape.

The second the screen flickered back into life, every zombie in the room snapped to attention, drawing closer and closer to the television and the happy sounds of love and friendship.

Steph watched on the other side of the crowd of zombies as Chris and Lisa examined each other's bites. There were tears in their eyes but they weren't crying for themselves, she realized, they were crying for each other. On the TV, Steph saw herself, lying in the ball pit at Thunderballs, right before they discovered Mrs. Hinzmann.

"Show us some human interest," Chris called behind the camera, laughter in his voice.

On the screen, someone she remembered from what felt like a thousand years ago grinned awkwardly as he snickered.

"Are you making a video?" TV Steph shouted back as Chris dissolved into a puddle of giggles. *"You asshole."*

Clinging to her chisel, she desperately tried to think of a way out of this. Maybe they could come with her, maybe there was a cure, and if she just kept them safe or tied up or locked in a closet or something.

But Chris knew it was too late. He felt the same burning in his arm as Lisa. He felt his blood heating up. He wanted to scream but he couldn't. All he could do was stay still and stay quiet and wait for Steph to get away. He pulled Lisa close for a hug and she rested her damp face on his chest, and then, with his best smile, he raised his hand and softly waved good-bye to his newest friend.

Tears ran down Steph's cheeks. It wasn't fair. It wasn't right. She raised her own hand to wave back, forcing herself not to run over there and murder everyone in the room. He deserved so much more than a wave, but if she didn't leave now, before . . . The alternative didn't bear thinking about. Adjusting the strap of her satchel, she turned, her heart breaking into a thousand different pieces with every step she took, until she was out in the silent hallway, the door closed shut behind her. All she could do now was find Anna and Nick and hope against hope that she wasn't the last woman alive.

✦ ✦ ✦

In the staff room, Chris's videos played on. He stroked Lisa's hair, even as his arm grew heavy and stiff.

"What'd you think?" he asked, nodding toward his film playing on the TV screen.

"I love it," she said, her voice full of trembling emotion.

"Imagine if we'd never met," Chris whispered, his voice cracking with the effort of making words. They weren't coming so easily now.

"But we did," Lisa replied. "And it was amazing."

He looked down at her beautiful face, devastated that he couldn't save her, but so happy to not be alone in all of this. There was relief and at last, no more fear. A tear spilled out of his eye and landed on Lisa's face as they turned back to face the TV and waited.

26

ANNA HAD NEVER been a massive fan of Christmas songs. They were always cheesy, overproduced, and usually super derivative. There was no originality left in Christmas. Well, except for maybe this one. She stalked slowly through the deserted hallways, following the jingle bells of a jaunty, festive tune all the way to the school auditorium. The music grew louder as she pushed open the door, impaling a zombie with the business end of her candy cane and tossing him down to the floor without so much as a second thought.

It had been a rough couple of days.

The hall was still set up for the Christmas show. She brushed her wild hair away from her face, looking down at her blood-spattered shirt, her bruised knuckles. She looked as though *she* had been part of a show. This couldn't possibly be real life. Between herself and the stage were a sea of zombies, all staring straight ahead, jaws slack and making happy, satisfied little groaning noises. In the middle of the stage, fully lit with a turkey leg in one hand and a bottle of wine in the other, was Savage. Behind him, tied tightly to a chair and wrapped in strings of lights, was her dad.

Anna stayed hidden in the shadows, her heart pounding with something she had almost forgotten. She was so afraid he was already gone, that Savage had done something terrible to her poor dad, but there he was, battered and bloody but definitely alive and definitely still human. She glanced around the room, taking stock of the situation. The fire exits had been boarded up, and there were stacks of boxes and chairs blocking the stage exits. This was the only way in and out of the auditorium. One way or another, she had to get through the swarm of zombies, free her dad, and get back out again without either of them getting bitten.

"Ah, Mr. Price." Savage took a huge bite out of his turkey leg and grinned as a student Anna recognized from the year below crawled across the stage in a torn magician's costume. "Bet you wish you hadn't keyed my car now, don't you?"

"I've told you," he gasped, reaching the edge of the stage and finding a barricade of piled-up desks, chairs, and tables between himself and the horde. "It wasn't me!"

"Do you have any proof that it wasn't you? Any alibi?" Savage asked, dropping his turkey leg into Tony's lap and grabbing the boy by his collar. "Because I'm almost certain that it was."

"I didn't," the boy sobbed. "I swear it."

Savage shrugged, braced himself, and hurled the screaming teen into the audience. Anna shrank back as the zombies surged onto the offering, muffling his screams with slobbering groans. Waiting until they were all distracted, Anna crept down the aisle, keeping low, candy cane close at hand.

"Why are you doing this, Arthur?" Tony screamed. There were no students left. Savage had been playing judge, jury, and executioner ever since he opened the doors and let these evil things in, and now there was only the two of them left.

"Did you not hear me?" Savage replied, picking up his turkey leg and resuming his meal. "He keyed my car. Actually, I don't think he did but he really pissed me off with that shoddy magic act in the Christmas show and honestly, I just didn't like the look of him."

"That doesn't make sense," Tony muttered, watching

as Price's top hat sailed across the crowd before settling on the head of a zombie lunch lady.

"Doesn't it?" Savage spun around and grabbed his nemesis by the chin. "Then how about this? I'm doing it because I can."

He slapped Tony hard around the face and went back to his wine and turkey. If he'd been asked to list his wildest fantasies, sending the entire population of the school to their untimely death by way of a zombie invasion wouldn't have even made the top ten, but it was like people said, he sighed, looking out at the blank, bloody faces in front of him. You never really knew yourself until you were faced with a crisis.

Deep in the middle of the audience, Anna stopped, crouching low as she saw the empty, dead eyes of the magician staring back at her through the zombie's legs. Transferring her candy cane to the other hand, she kept on going. Up on the stage, Tony saw something move while Savage carried on with his lunch. He stiffened against his ropes—it wasn't possible, was it? Trying not to attract attention, he shook his head, staring Anna down with stern but watery eyes. But he knew his daughter; she was too determined to walk away, even if the price was her life.

Leaping to his feet, Savage spun the spotlight on the

edge of the stage, illuminating Anna right where she stood. He knew she was there. He'd spotted her the second she walked into the hall, but this was his school now, she was playing his game by his rules. And now she was stranded in the middle of a sea of zombies, in the perfect position for her precious dad to watch her be ripped to shreds.

"How are you not dead yet?" he crooned, leaning his elbows on the spotlight.

"I don't know," Anna said, ducking as the first zombie lunged her way. "Probably because you're as shit at this as you are at your job."

"Run, love!" Tony yelled as his daughter plunged the sharp end of her candy cane right into the zombie's face. Anna rose to her feet, standing tall as her victim collapsed to the floor. She fixed Savage with a smile and cracked her neck.

"Is that all you've got?" she asked, Nick's cocky words ringing in her ears.

Savage sighed, examining his nails.

"Still a show-off, I see," he said with a yawn. "Well, go on then, give us a show."

He bolted across the stage, spinning every single light until they were all on Anna, and then, to really make sure the zombies were paying attention, he cranked the music as loud as it would go.

Anna took a deep breath, calmly set her candy cane down, and using both hands, she carefully wrapped her hair into a ponytail as if she was preparing for an entirely new war. She picked the candy cane up again and braced herself. She wasn't afraid to fight, not anymore. One after another, the zombies attacked, leaping, lunging, clawing, and swiping, every one of them meeting their end as Anna fought back with newfound strength. She ducked out of the way as one zombie parent flew at her, tipping him over with the hook of her candy cane and watching as he landed on his head, his neck snapped at a sickening angle.

"Oh, Miss Shepherd." Savage leaned against the spotlight, moving it around the room as he followed Anna in her explosion of violence. "You don't understand. A purge on this species is long overdue. We're done, we're broken. We brought this entirely on ourselves. Fighting is futile! The way I look at it, we're already dead, so why not have a cheeky bit of fun?"

"A cheeky bit of fun?" Anna asked, yanking her weapon out of the chest cavity of a particularly foul-smelling former fireman. "You murdered John's mom!"

"Did I?" he screamed back, suddenly completely unhinged. Just as quickly as he'd lost it, he regained his composure and smiled. "No wait, you're right, I did. Guess what? You're up next."

"Then I'll give you one hell of a show," Anna yelled back. "You won't want to miss this, Savage."

Behind him, Tony wrestled with his bonds, his skin burning as he struggled against the ropes that were bound so tightly around his wrists.

On the floor, Anna grabbed a fire extinguisher and sprayed the school crossing lady and her husband in the face before finishing them off with one hard crack from her bloodstained candy cane. Bringing it back around for another swipe, she felt the cane hook against something. It was her dad's friend Jerry, caught in the crook and gnashing his teeth in her direction. With all her might, Anna spun herself and the cane around in a circle, sending Jerry flying into a gaggle of zombified parents.

"You're a silly wee girl," Savage crowed as he leaned over the edge of the stage to bait her with his psychotic and insulting banter.

"And you're a madman!" Anna shouted back, leaping onto a chair to get a clear view of his manic, ginger face.

He acknowledged her accusation with a cold, one-shouldered shrug.

"The truth can be hard to hear sometimes," he said, tipping his head to one side. "You say madman, I say evil genius. One looks so much better on a résumé than the other."

"How. Can. You. Take. Pleasure. In. This?" Anna

asked, punctuating every word by bludgeoning another zombie in the head.

"I've been taking a course in mindfulness," Savage replied. "I live in the now. I'd recommend it if you weren't about to die."

"Anna!"

Her dad shrieked her name as one of the zombies reached up and grabbed her ankle. Anna fell hard, cracking her head on the edge of a wooden bench.

Everything went dark.

"Ooh, this is the good bit," Savage said, clapping and jumping up and down on the spot. "Are you watching, Shepherd? I'd hate for you to miss your daughter's *denouement*."

Anna moaned as the light from Savage's spotlight blurred her vision, a heavy thumping sound filling her ears as a shadow reared up over her head. She was down, but not out. Feeling around for her candy cane, she found a handful of pencils instead and before she could even think about the grossness that followed, she jammed them up into the eyes of the zombie that lurched over her.

"Get up, Anna!" Tony yelled, still fighting against his ropes. He pushed and pulled while Anna grabbed for her weapon, toppling his chair over with his escape efforts.

From his vantage point on the stage, Savage did not like what he saw. She was supposed to be dead by now, but here she was, leading the bloody zombies in what looked just like an undead ceilidh dance.

"It's a sad day when you can't even trust zombies to get the job done," he snarled. "If you want something done right and all that . . ."

"Get! Down!" Anna screamed, beating a row of zombies down onto the floor, pausing only to kick one square in the crown jewels. She hadn't really expected it to work, but he collapsed, just like John had that one time she accidentally-on-purpose kicked him in the nuts after he made fun of her Girl Guide uniform when she was thirteen. The fallen zombies created a path, leading all the way up to the stage.

"Oh, hang on a minute." Savage's eyes opened excitedly as he realized what Anna was planning to do. Truly he was going to get his Christmas wish after all. "Come on, Miss Shepherd!" he shouted. "I'm waiting!"

Taking a deep breath, she shook her head at her own idea and then pelted full speed through a narrow opening in the horde, springing off the back of a bent-over zombie she had spotted eating something on the floor near the stage, leaping over the barricades, and landing on the stage in a heap beside her dad.

Arthur staggered backward, unable to believe it had worked. He watched as Anna sliced her candy cane through the bindings that held her dad, fighting with the ropes and the Christmas lights, while the undead roused themselves on the auditorium floor beneath them.

Anna squeezed her dad so tightly, a burning pain shooting through her knee where she'd landed on it. Tony worried that she might crack one of his ribs she was squeezing so hard, and he'd never been so grateful. The look on his face, the pride in his eyes. She couldn't think of a moment when she'd ever been happier. Until her dad stood up, turned around, and slugged Savage right in the gut.

"Leave him," Anna said as they towered over the fallen man. "He doesn't matter. Not to anyone."

"You get back here!" Savage croaked from his prone position on the floor. He would not be abandoned, he would not be ignored. They would stay and they would watch and they would do as they were told. But Anna and Tony were already onto the next task, pulling apart the barricaded exits at the side of the stage.

"NO!" Savage screamed, any and all thoughts of zombies forgotten. He grabbed the neck of his wine bottle and smashed it against the leg of a chair. He'd make them pay attention, he'd make them listen to him one way or another.

He sprinted right at Anna, and she turned with her candy cane, ready to swat him out of the way like the insignificant idiot he was, but instead, her dad barged right in front of her, intercepted Savage, and threw him to the ground. The two men rolled around the stage, crashing into lights, fighting over the broken bottle. Below, the zombies were awake, and they were angry. With missing arms and legs, they began to mount the barricades, no longer distracted by Savage's lights and music, only one thing in mind.

Anna stood watching as Savage and her father rose to their feet, Tony right on the edge of the stage, only inches away from the snapping jaws of the horde.

"Oh, Tony," Savage laughed. "Looks like I'll have to finish you off and then your daughter. Sorry to disappoint."

But Anna had other plans. The giant star that hung suspended in midair, above the middle of the stage, swayed ever so slightly with all the action below. She dove across the stage and grabbed the end of the rope that held it fast, untying it as quickly as her chapped and bloody hands would allow.

"DAD!" she yelled, pointing up at the stage ceiling as she let go of the rope. The north star swung down from its resting place and Tony dropped to his knees, ducking out of the way. But Arthur Savage did not see it coming. He turned at the last moment, a look of complete surprise on his face as the star slammed him right in the chest and sent him sailing through the air, right into the open arms of his audience of zombies.

"They love me!" he cried as they crowd-surfed him along on their hands. Tony crawled back to Anna, a look of horror on his face. "They really love me!"

And then he disappeared. Consumed by the crowd, eaten up by the very zombies he'd let into the school. His screams split through the Christmas music and the rabid moans and groans as Anna and her dad held on to each other on the stage.

"We've got to go," she said, grabbing her dad's hand, ready to help him to his feet. "They'll be done with him in a second, we don't have any time."

Tony didn't move. Instead, he rolled up his trouser leg to reveal an angry bite mark, already throbbing and turning purple. He looked up at a grief-stricken Anna with tears in his eyes.

"I'm sorry, love," he whispered. "I'm so sorry."

"No!" Anna screamed. "No, no, no!"

She turned away from her father and took her candy cane to the set of the Christmas show, battering Santa's house, crushing the North Pole, kicking prop presents across the stage.

"Come here," Tony said, wrapping his daughter up in a calming hug. Their last hug. "You need to leave."

"They've got to be working on a cure," Anna whispered. She dropped her candy cane to the floor, all the fight ebbing out of her.

"It happens too quickly," Tony said. Thanks to Savage, he'd seen the change happen more times than he could count. "I can't come with you."

Anna looked up into her father's eyes and saw herself

reflected. This whole time, her only plan was to find him. And now she was lost.

"I don't know what to do," she confessed through a river of tears.

"Yes, you do. You always do," Tony corrected. He swept her hair out of her face and dried her eyes with his thumbs. "God, Anna. If only your mum could see you now."

As they stared at each other—Anna trying hard to find some semblance of strength, and Tony feeling nothing but love and pride—one of the barricaded exits burst open. Nick stood in the doorway, baseball bat in hand, absolutely drenched in blood. He looked at Anna and smiled before registering the expression on her face. The tears in her eyes. The wound on Tony's leg.

"I can't say I'm crazy about your boyfriend," Tony commented, giving Nick his patented warning look. It might be the end of the world, but he was still the father of a teenage girl.

"He's not my boyfriend," Anna said, laughing at the absurdity of it all. Nick was alive, her father was dying, they'd just fed the assistant principal to a bunch of zombies, and here she was, talking about her love life.

"Oh, well, there's some good news," Tony replied before hissing with pain. His leg began to burn. "You need to go. Now."

"But I don't want to," Anna said in a small, girlish voice.

"Love." He grabbed her hand and looked at his daughter with imploring eyes. "For once in your life, don't argue with me."

"Savage said something about Julie not turning . . ." she muttered, looking down at the floor. "Do—do you want me to . . . help?"

"No, don't," Nick said, his face pleading, having lived through exactly what she was implying and not wanting the same for Anna.

"He's right," Tony agreed. He might not be able to save her from this reality, but he could spare her of that memory. "I'm so proud of you, Anna Elizabeth Shepherd." He continued, giving her one last squeeze, savoring the moment. "Now, bugger off. You've got places to go."

His face tightened with pain and Anna watched as the color started to drain from his face. Gently, Nick pulled on her arm. They needed to be somewhere else, and fast.

"Merry Christmas, Dad," she whispered with a smile. Her last gift to him.

"Merry Christmas, Anna," he replied, nodding to Nick before taking one last look at his girl.

With Nick guiding the way, Anna stumbled out of the hall, leaving the chaos and her father behind, blinded by the flood of tears that streamed down her cheeks.

On the stage, Tony watched her go. His brave, bold, clever only child. Her mother's double. He slumped backward, finally crying out with pain when he was certain she was out of earshot. The last thing he needed was for her to come back and see him like this. Silently, he pulled his phone out of his pocket and pressed the home button. A photo of himself, Liz, and Anna shone brightly in the gloom. Anna's mother, the love of his life.

"I'll be with you soon, love," he whispered as he closed his eyes.

✦ ✦ ✦

Outside the school was even more terrifying than Anna remembered. She limped out into the parking lot at Nick's side as the sky began to shift from night into day.

It was Christmas morning and they needed a miracle.

"Have you seen Steph?" she asked, testing her weight on her injured knee. It didn't feel great but she could stand. Nick shook his head, mute.

"Chris? Lisa?"

"I'm sorry," he said, shaking his head, unable to vocalize what he'd seen in the staff room. He gripped his bloody baseball bat tightly.

Anna understood, but filed the news away to deal with later. There would be time to grieve for John, for

Julie, for Chris and Lisa, and her dad, and everyone. But for now, they still had to fight. She followed Nick's gaze and raised her candy cane. There were more of them. Of course there were more of them. Zombies lined up behind the school fence, pouring through the gaps one at a time. Others appeared behind them, spilling out of the building and filling the lot around them.

"Oh, Nick," she sighed, pressing her back against his as they turned in slow circles, trying to watch every angle.

"It's just a couple of zombies," he replied. "What's new?"

Anna looked up, the sound of banging coming from the door they had just closed behind them. As if the current situation wasn't bad enough, it burst open and every zombie teacher, parent, and student joined the mass of undead bodies that surrounded them.

"There's still hope," Anna said, grim determination in her voice.

"Whatever you say," Nick said, readying himself for the fight. "All I know is, if I'm going down, I'm taking as many of these fuckers with me as possible."

The first wave of zombies attacked.

Back-to-back, they fought with every ounce of strength in their bodies. When Nick fell, she picked him up, when Anna stumbled, he had her back. Anna panted, twirling her candy cane in her hands as the zombies regrouped.

Nick yelled as he tripped over a headless zombie, landing hard on his arm. She looked over and saw him cradling the injury, panic in his blue eyes. With a leap and a cry, Anna plunged the end of her candy cane into the zombie bearing down on Nick, dropping it to the floor.

"Are you bitten?" she asked, the two of them taking a moment to catch their breath.

Nick shook his head. "But they're going to keep coming."

Anna nodded. He was right, they were. Nick tried to rise to his feet, but there was nothing left in him. His legs wouldn't do what his brain demanded. Instead, he dropped any remaining hope as yet more zombies appeared on the horizon, illuminated by the coming dawn.

"I'm sorry," he said, completely defeated as he sat on the ground, unable to stand. Anna stood over him and looked down with a tired smile.

"Yeah," she said, still not quite ready to give up.

The zombies were circling, dragging it out, making her wait, when she felt something cold on the tip of her nose. It was snowing. Chris was getting his white

Christmas after all. Anna tilted her face skyward, smiling as the snowflakes began to fall faster, clinging to her eyebrows and eyelashes. She thought of John, her best friend in the world. She thought of Chris and Lisa and Steph and how brave people could be when it really mattered. She thought of her mom, missing her with all her heart, but so pleased she'd never had to live through this nightmare, and she thought of her dad. Her brilliant, wonderful, loving dad. She'd lost so much, had given so much, and now she was done. The candy cane slipped out of her fingers and rattled on the concrete as she fell to the ground, leaning against Nick.

The zombies staggered forward. The finality of their menacing roar and gnashing teeth inching ever closer. And then, not far away, a car horn honked. And honked again. Anna and Nick looked up in unison to see Steph's car appear around the corner.

Honking the horn as she tore through the crowds, Steph mowed down swathes of zombies to get to her friends.

The car skidded to a stop next to Anna and Nick, and the window rolled down. "The roads were a little blocked, so I had to go around," she explained unnecessarily. "Get in!"

Anna yanked at Nick as they scrambled to their feet and tugged on the door handles.

"Open the bloody doors!" Nick yelled as the fallen zombies clawed at their legs.

Steph frowned. "Sorry."

She pressed a button and the door flew open. Nick and Anna jumped inside. Anna reached for the handle and yanked the door shut as Steph tore off out of the parking lot, knocking down zombies like bowling pins as she went. She looked back over her shoulder as they zoomed out of the school driveway and out onto the street. She wiped away the only tears she had left in her, took a deep breath, and closed her eyes.

"Boom! Saved your life," Steph said trying to lighten things up. "Although I hate to think what they've done to my paintwork. D'you think my insurance will cover it? Or is zombie invasion considered an act of God?"

Anna couldn't help but manage an exhausted half smile as Nick grabbed his seat belt and fastened it over his bloody clothes, his baseball bat rolling around in the footwell. She pushed herself up onto her knees and watched as the school got smaller and smaller through the back window.

"So," Steph said, glancing down at the fuel gauge. Full tank for the win. "Where to?"

Nick immediately opened his mouth to answer and then paused. He had no idea. Instead, he looked over at Anna as she turned around and rested her head back, finally allowing herself to relax. They'd lost so much, she realized, staring up at the soft beige roof of the car. Their families, their friends, their futures, but they still had one another. She looked at Nick and then at Steph and then out the window as Little Haven disappeared and the open road beckoned.

"I don't know," Anna said, leaning forward between the seats to turn on the car radio and give Steph a determined look. "But we'll figure it out. Together."

ACKNOWLEDGMENTS

You think taking the perfect selfie is hard? Try writing a book! It takes a village, and I am so incredibly blessed and grateful to have an amazing village that contributed to making the *Anna and the Apocalypse* novel a reality. Starting with the huh-mazing Lindsey Kelk, who was my mentor, editing conscience, and friend. I simply adore you. Erin Stein and I started our journey in 2010 when we partnered on the very first Monster High book—and it is so good to be reunited—thank you, thank you, thank you for all your support. I cannot wait until you, Lindsey, and I are in the same place at the same time to have a celebration.

This book would never have happened had it not been for Alan McDonald, a scholar of words and a supreme magician when it comes to knowing how to put them together. Your and Ryan McHenry's masterful work on writing the *Anna and the Apocalypse* screenplay was the best guiding light that anyone could hope for, and I am forever grateful for your amazing words, many of which are included herein, since why mess with perfection? My boys Roddy Hart and Tommy Reilly, who are the two most talented composers in the world and kindly allowed me to include "The Fish Wrap" and "It's that Time of Year" lyrics in the book. A shout-out to Blazing Griffin's Catriona Ewen, contract ninja, and Peter van der Watt for their support. Thank you to my story guides and historians, Naysun Alae-Carew, Nic Crum, and Gillian Christie, there is so much more to come.

I also need to express the impact the talented film actors had on this story. Each one perfectly bringing to life their character so well that it was impossible to write this without them in my head. Ella Hunt, Malcolm Cumming, Sarah Swire, Marli Siu, Christopher Leveaux, and Ben Wiggins, you are a wonderful, crazy family now and I am so looking forward to watching your stars rise high in the heavens. The brilliant Paul Kaye and magnanimous Mark Benton, you are simply . . . the . . . best.

Finally, thank you to director John McPhail, and all the rest of his cast and crew that brought the screenplay to life on film, and are what gave shape to the story in these pages.

I can't wait for what's next!

—Barry Waldo